CHAMISA DREAMS

A Novel by R. B. Salter

SUNSTONE
PRESS

Santa Fe
New Mexico

Cover illustration by Beth Evans

First Edition

Printed in the United States of America

Library of Congress Cataloging—in—Publication Data:

Salter, Robert B., 1952-
    Chamisa dreams / Robert B. Salter, —1st ed.
       p. cm.
    ISBN: 0-86534-220-2 : $12.95
    1. Uranium miners—New Mexico—Health and hygiene—Fiction.
    2. Indians of North America—New Mexico—Fiction. 3. Navajo Indians—
    Fiction. I. Title.
    PS3569. A462246C53 1994
    813' .54—dc20   94-6780
                                                 CIP

Published by   Sunstone Press
                    Post Office Box 2321
                    Santa Fe, NM 87504-2321 / USA
                    (505) 988-4418 / orders only (800) 243-5644
                    FAX (505) 988-1025

INTRODUCTION

The four corners area of the United States has harbored a greater continuum of human civilization than any other region of the Americas, north of Mexico. The human culture has flourished in this area in spite of a difficult geographic and climatic circumstance. The people who first learned to live in this rugged land developed a keen sense of the carrying capacity of the land. They produced crops and hunted in the best of times in a somewhat sustainable fashion. And when the land was finally worn out their numbers across the countryside were not so great as to prevent migration into new, productive areas.

And so it was for a millenia or two in the high empty country of the Four Corners. The eb and flow of countless seasons and the times of bounty and hunger shaped the thinking of the people, and those thoughts gave birth to art and religion. Out of these high, original thoughts came some of the finest ceramics, and most impressive architectural works on the planet. And also out of this thought, influenced by nature, we have seen in a continuum to this day, a complex ritual framework that touches every aspect of life and the universe.

Into this realm of spirit life, the consumptive force of western Europe collided a few hundred years ago. Things have never been the same, but the original people managed to hold on to some very important pieces of their culture. It is the knowledge of nature's way that has so far brought the people through the brutal changes of the twentieth century.

Around the middle of this century the greatest assault ever against land and the people who live closest to it was launched with the discovery of uranium in the rocks of the four corners. The need for this hot rock was to fuel the development of an armaments race, to develop weapons that if used, would assure the destruction of the planet.

It was as if the whole world had gone crazy. The original people tending sheep and cattle in the area area around Mt. Taylor, New Mexico watched in amazement as strange white men with odd equipment burrowed deep into the earth or gouged out new canyons with their giant shovels. Many of them eagerly accepted jobs with the new mines and mills in this area where cash had previously seldom been seen.

Many things changed for the Navajo and Pueblo people when the companies and their allies in government came to the sacred mountain of the south. Roads were paved for the first time. Reliable water systems were installed. Education and medical care became more available. Values changed too. For some people, especially the young, the rituals necessary to obtain dollars became more important than the cycle of rituals required to insure rain and crops.

Another insidious and horrible change began to be noticed in Indian country by the 1970s. Dr. Laura Shields, at the Navajo Community College in Shiprock, New Mexico began to collect health data on uranium miners and their families and others who lived near mines and mills. She found an alarming rate of birth deformaties, still births, and cancer deaths among Navajos with some family connection to mining or living near uranium facilities.

To date no effort had been made by any public health agency to determine the effects of daily exposure to dangerous radioactive materials for the Navajo miners. Even at the time of this writing, more than ten years after the demise of the uranium boom, very little has been done to correct the great wrong done to the original people and the land in the four corners.

This process of overwhelming original cultures and taking from their land base all that the industrial-consumptive dominant culture wants, continues, even as you read. The original people who carry on with their simple lives and ready contact with the infinite in the face of such overwhelming odds are the inspiration for CHAMISA DREAMS.

Without them we have no one to show us the way to live in peace with this small planet.

–R. B. *Salter*
Santa Fe, 1994

CHAPTER I - ONWARD TO CABEZON

Jed Flyway crushed another empty can of Tecate and tossed it into a substantial pile of similar containers that neatly filled the floorboard on the passenger side of his ramshackle '52 Willys pick- up.

Jed thrust his hand into the slightly cool liquid contents of a sizable ice chest on the seat beside him. He ran his hand thoughtfully and slowly around the inside of the container while observing the highway in as careful a manner as one who has ingested a great quantity of beer can. Finally his groping hand made contact with the last remaining can of Tecate.

"Shit . . . the last fucking beer!" he exclaimed loudly, as though some unseen inventory agent were making notes.

Jed squirmed uneasily in his seat as he opened his last can of refreshment. He took a deep and anxious gulp that lowered its contents by nearly half.

Jed's antsy behavior was largely due to a pressing and common biological need. He needed to pee, bad. Jed had been acutely aware of this need for at least the last 47 miles. He had passed up plenty of opportunities to safely and discreetly relieve himself. For over two hours Jed had been traveling through quite remote country on the edge of the San Juan Basin in Northern New Mexico.

But Jed Flyway had a mission, a destination in mind, and he was determined to postpone the inevitable until he reached a very special point along the road. Jed was swallowing the last gulp of his last beer when he spied the turnoff into a highway rest area less than a mile ahead. By this time he was able to think of little more than his imminent need.

Jed leapt out of his still moving truck as it rolled slowly past the sign marking the Continental Divide.

Jed's truck sputtered to a halt a few feet from where he stood frantically trying to lower his fly and release the deluge.

"Ahhhh, blessed relief. Thank you Lord," was Jed's heartfelt expression to the universe as he experienced that un-comparable release of pressure, apparently un-aware of the presence of several shocked elderly couples resting themselves and their travel trailers at the same highway rest area.

Jed was quick to notice that more of the runoff was headed for the Gulf of Mexico than the Pacific and he made rapid adjustments in position to compensate for this injustice. As usual Jed stood for quite a while after draining his bladder, admiring his contribution to North American hydrology.

Finally with a deep feeling of satisfaction Jed zipped his jeans and strolled with a smile to his waiting vehicle. With a cheerful greeting and a waive to his stunned audience he rolled out of the rest area and onto Highway 44 westbound.

Jed proceeded through the sagebrush and badlands for several miles until he reached the Seven Springs Bar and Trading Post where he replenished his ice chest with a case of Dos Equis beer.

As Jed proceeded on his journey he turned off the paved highway onto a dirt track reservation road and began to take note of his advanced state of inebriation. His muddled thoughts turned to Lucy Begay, the Navajo woman he was on his way to visit. Lucy lived near Torreon on the checkerboard lands with her grandparents. She was home for a visit from Utah State University.

Lucy and Jed met during a raft trip down the San Juan River the previous summer. They were quite casual lovers really, having seen each other only twice in the previous three months. This had been characteristic of Jed's way of life for many years. After surviving the sixties in Northern New Mexico with lovers coming and going like dust devils, he had convinced himself that his freedom and sanity depended on not getting too close to anyone. Jed had, up till this point, loved primarily his work as a contract archaeologist and had considered his human relationships an aside to life rather than the center.

But even Jed had to admit there was something special and different about Lucy Begay. Jed began to feel bad that after six weeks of separation Lucy would now see him in his present, less than optimum condition. He determined that he had to eat something and sober up a little before driving out to the tiny cluster of hogans and corrals north of Cabezon where Lucy was.

Jed veered down a side track toward Torreon seeking sustenance and a degree of sobriety. Jed halted his vehicle in Torreon and staggered into Hostene George's Honky Tonk, Pool Hall and Snack Bar.

The dimly lit interior of Hostene George's place was full of large dark Navajo shapes that stopped their indistinguishable chatter only long enough to take a quick glance at this belagana stranger invading their remote world. The Navajo din quickly resumed to the accompaniment of an old Hank Williams tune on the jukebox. Several couples danced slowly, shuffling cheek to cheek to the scratchy old record.

Most of the Indians in the bar sat still as death in alcoholic stupor not unlike Jed's own present condition. One old man offered Jed a Budweiser.

"Oh God no," Jed moaned pushing away the bottle. "No hostene . . . thank you no . . . I'm already bad drunk . . . I need to eat something."

"No problem Joe," the old man responded. "Hostene George'll get you some good groceries." The old man belched and laughed. "Yea brutter, that old hostene he got some good stew on the stove . . . and fry bread and coffee."

Jed indicated with gestures that the suggested entrees sounded adequate.

The old man pulled Jed by the sleeve to a corner of the bar where several rusted tubular steel chairs were scattered around an empty oil drum.

With a grunt and a gesture he indicated that Jed was to sit. "I help you no? You buy me drink now?"

"Sure." Jed answered slowly. "But where do I get the stew?"

The old man took Jed's dollar and pointed with his lips to a stocky middle aged Navajo lady leaning back precariously against the bar in a folding chair.

Jed approached the reclining woman and spoke politely. "Excuse me ma'am but I'd like some stew and bread and coffee . . . please."

The woman did not respond. In fact she didn't seem to be conscious and the dark glasses she wore inside the darkened bar made determining her state of being very difficult. Jed was about to begin his request again when the woman reached up her hand and raised her dark glasses.

"You want some of hostene George's stew?" she asked with a tone of disbelief.

"Uh . . . yes ma'am," Jed answered. "I sure do. And some frybread and coffee."

The woman began to chuckle as she struggled to her feet. "Ok belagana . . . I'll get your food." She continued to chuckle as she waddled off to a small room in the corner of the bar. She seemed to be barely containing her laughter when she returned in a few minutes with a tray containing the sustenance Jed had requested.

"Three dollars belagana," she said with a broad Navajo smile. Jed handed her the money and settled in at the oil drum table to what smelled like the best green chile mutton stew he had ever encountered. The chile was hot to be sure, but Jed liked good flavorful hot chile.

He was nearly halfway through with the bowl before he realized that this chile was hot at first and became progressively hotter as it moved into and through his gastro-intestinal tract. By the time Jed wiped up the last vestige of stew with his frybread and gulped down the last drop of coffee he felt as though a blast furnace was operating in his body cavity.

As Jed entered the bright afternoon sun he realized that although he had successfully warded off his drunkenness his vision was strangely blurred and his ears were ringing. To make matters worse Jed's bowels were churning like high tide surf at Big Sur.

As Jed bounced on down the road toward Lucy's grandparent's place he was suddenly taken with an overpowering urge to both defecate and vomit. He jumped out of his truck and ran into the chamisa alongside the road and attempted to accomplish both functions simultaneously.

Jed was a complete mess after this episode and he decided a bath was in order. He noticed a windmill several hundred feet off the road and headed for it totally naked with clothes in hand. Shortly before he reached his objective a pick-up truck loaded with Navajo kids roared down the road with the occupants hooting and yelling, "Hey white ass!"

Jed ignored this indignity and walked on toward the stock tank at the base of the windmill. After a few minutes of serious washing Jed looked and felt somewhat better despite his wounded dignity and aching head. It had been quite a day of drinking and driving and eating Hostene George's deadly chile mutton stew. Now Jed felt he was ripe for Lucy's special touch and he proceeded toward his destination with that goal in mind.

As Jed shut down his vehicle in front of a well kept log hogan he was very pleased to see Lucy emerge from the door with blankets in hand. He looked at her long black hair and smiled as he thought of the close evening he expected.

"How are you Lucy?" he asked as he leaned out of the truck window to hug her.

"Hello Jed, you smell like shit," she replied pushing him away. "Here, take these blankets and sleep in your truck. I'll explain tomorrow. And take a bath at the tank."

Jed didn't have time to respond before Lucy disappeared back into the hogan. He did take another bath and this time with soap. When he was finally clean and in fresh clothes Jed stretched out in the back of his truck under the surreal New Mexico night sky and drifted off to a much needed sleep.

Jed awoke in the pre-dawn darkness to the muffled sounds of Lucy's grandparents shuffling past his truck. He watched them quietly for a few moments as they walked to a neatly stacked pile of flat stones a short distance from their hogan.

They knelt together in prayer as the first hint of light appeared over the Nacimiento Mountains. Jed drifted from this scene back into a dream filled sleep that ceased only when Lucy shook him to wakefulness in the full light of morning.

"You smell a little better now Jed." She whispered leaning over the truck bed where Jed lay.

Jed rubbed his eyes and pushed back his hair as he sat up. "What's going on Lucy?" he asked squinting into the sun. "Why couldn't we be together last night?"

"Its a long story," Lucy replied quietly. "I'll tell you after we eat something."

"Not chile mutton stew I hope," Jed mumbled.

"No. Why, have you developed a fear of stew?"

"Never mind," Jed answered. "That's a long story too and I don't think I'll ever tell it to you." Lucy smiled and went back into the hogan. In a few minutes Lucy returned carrying a steaming piece of frybread and a battered tin cup full of hot, strong smelling coffee.

"See if you can deal with this white man." Lucy was smiling as she handed Jed his breakfast.

Jed handled this meal quite well and as he wiped his face with a turquoise bandana he asked again, "Now, tell me what's going on."

Lucy looked away toward the distant San Mateo Mountains and whispered, "Let's walk." Jed nodded agreement and walked off slowly through the stunted sagebrush and overgrazed grass that surrounded Lucy's grandparent's place.

The couple walked silently for nearly a mile before Lucy suddenly turned toward Jed, hugged him, and began to sob deeply.

"What is it Lucy?" Jed asked trying to look at her face buried against his chest. "What's the matter?"

Lucy took a deep breath and looked up at Jed. "My sister's new baby died. It was horribly deformed at birth and lived only a few minutes." Lucy paused a few moments then bit her finger to control her tears before continuing. "My sister Rose is dying too, of grief and I think cancer." Lucy began to sob again and Jed held her tightly.

"I'm so sorry Lucy. This is a bad time for me to be here. I'll leave."

"No Jed no. I want you near me. I need you. I need for you to hold me and love me."

Jed looked down at the woman in his arms dazed by all he had just heard especially the part about love. He had always carefully avoided the use of that particular word and now in the midst of tragedy here it was.

At that moment Jed began to feel something he hadn't let himself feel for years. He was needed by someone and it felt good.

He kissed the top of Lucy's head and said, "All right darlin I'm here. I'll do whatever I can to help you. I'm right here."

Jed and Lucy walked quietly back to the hogan. Just before they reached the door Lucy turned to Jed and said, "Wait a minute here and let me see what's going on inside."

Lucy opened the door in a few minutes and motioned for Jed to enter. Jed proceeded nervously, not at all sure he was a welcome guest under the circumstances. At first Jed could see very little in the dim light of a single kerosene lamp. Finally as his eyes adjusted he could see that the space was shared by Lucy's grandparents and another old Navajo man sitting on the dirt floor beside the contorted body of Lucy's sister.

Rose was lying in a fetal position on top of an intricate sand painting. Only by looking very closely could Jed see that Rose was still breathing in a shallow and irregular fashion. Everyone in the hogan was completely silent except for the old man beside Rose. He was singing a soft and strange Navajo song.

As Jed watched the ancient healing ritual unfold he lost all consciousness of time. Hours passed as he watched Rose and the healer. The longer he watched the more he wondered why so much tragedy had been inflicted on one small Navajo woman.

Jed was gently drawn back to present time by a touch on the shoulder from Lucy. She motioned for him to follow and the two of them left the hogan. Outside Jed was surprised to see the brilliant colors of sunset. He had spent the entire afternoon transfixed by the drama of impending death.

Lucy reached into the bed of Jed's pick-up and grabbed one of the blankets there and walked off toward the sunset. Jed watched her dark willowy form silhouetted against the crimson sky for a moment then followed. Lucy walked down a sheep trail into a deep arroyo and spread the blanket carefully on the dry sandy channel.

She stood looking at Jed for what seemed to him a long time. Finally without a word she began to un-snap the buttons on her flannel shirt. Jed's breath became shallow and his heart quickened as she dropped her shirt in the sand. As Jed stood looking at Lucy in the fading sunset light she proceeded to remove her boots and jeans.

Even though his body was responding to Lucy, Jed's mind was racing. In spite of the beautiful woman obviously giving herself to him he could not forget the scene they had just left. Lucy's sister was dying and here 200 yards away she was standing naked in the rising moonlight in front of him. It didn't seem right to Jed.

He opened his mouth and tried to voice this feeling but Lucy raised a dark hand and stopped him.

"No!" she whispered. "This is what I want right now. I want to feel alive, right now before death comes to take my sister."

She ripped open the snaps on Jed's denim shirt and pulled herself tightly against his chest. Jed needed no further convincing of her sincerity. He kicked off his boots and dropped his jeans. The two lovers embraced in the moonlight and dropped onto the blanket.

For a while at least there was nothing but each other. Lucy and Jed lay locked in a sweaty embrace for hours, repeating the timeless dance of human lovers several times before an un-earthly sound brought them back to the world of others.

It was the piercing sound of an eagle bone whistle that caused Lucy to pull away from Jed and stand over him looking back toward the hogan.

"What was that?" Jed asked looking up at Lucy standing over him.

"That's the holy man announcing the arrival of death." Lucy quickly found her clothes and began to put them on.

"Come on Jed, come with me," Lucy said as she walked away leaving Jed still sprawled naked in the arroyo. Jed quickly pulled on his boots and jeans and was still buttoning his shirt when he arrived at the hogan and saw Lucy talking quietly to the holy man.

She turned to Jed and instructed him, "Get a blanket from your truck and help carry Rose outside."

Jed did not question the instructions for a moment for he knew that if anyone died inside the hogan of traditional Navajos like Lucy's grandparents the whole place and everything in it would be abandoned.

He quickly grabbed a blanket from his truck and followed the holy man into the hogan where Lucy's sister lay convulsing and breathing in short irregular gasps. Jed and the holy man spread the blanket beside the sand painting and gently moved Rose on to it. The holy man picked up an eagle feather fan and quickly but carefully erased all traces of the sand painting. The old man then covered Rose in the blanket and motioned for Jed to carry her outside.

Jed paused outside for a moment and looked to the old man for some indication of which way to go. The holy man pointed with his lips to the stone shrine Jed had watched Lucy's grandparents pray at the previous morning. Jed and the old man walked past the shrine to the crest of a small rise where a tiny bundle wrapped in an old rug was lying.

The holy man indicated with a shrug and a grunt that this was the place to leave Rose. As Jed stood watching the holy man pulled his eagle bone whistle from a small pouch and blew four long shrill blasts on it. Afterward, the old man sauntered away as though his job was done. Jed could not take his eyes off Rose's convulsing body. He stood alone beside her for what may have been hours watching helplessly as she struggled with her impending death.

Suddenly with a strong convulsion and a gasp she grew quiet and Jed knew the end had finally come. Jed folded the blanket over the tortured face and walked away from Rose and the smaller bundle which he assumed was her baby. When Jed returned to the hogan the door was closed and there was no sound from within. He figured the truck was his appropriate bed again and he climbed in wearily to a night of more thought than sleep.

Jed woke the next morning to the sound of a slamming car door. He sat up in the bed of his truck and shook hands with the Mormon Bishop from Farmington. He had heard about the deaths from the holy man's family and had come to take the two bodies away for a decent Christian burial. Jed helped the Bishop load the small bundles into his station wagon.

He watched in stunned disbelief over the events of the last day as the Bishop disappeared in a cloud of dust. Jed was still watching the dust settle and thinking when Lucy came out of the hogan with another steaming frybread breakfast.

"How are you this morning?" Lucy asked, gently touching Jed's forehead.

"All right," Jed answered quietly. "A little tired but all right."

"Good," Lucy said brushing back Jed's hair with her fingers. "Thanks for being there last night."

Jed smiled and nodded his head. He devoured his breakfast and thought a few minutes about all that had happened. Finally he held Lucy by the shoulders and asked, "Can we take a walk today? A long walk. I want to talk to you about some things. About us, and about what happened here to Rose and her baby."

Lucy rocked on the high heels of her riding boots and looked into the sky then turned to Jed and answered, "Sure, we can take a walk. That would be fine. I'll try to answer your questions. And I have a few for you too. I'll get some carne seca, you grab your canteen."

Lucy stepped back into the hogan to get the food and Jed retrieved a battered blanket canteen from behind the seat of his pick-up. Jed and Lucy were soon walking south under the brilliant morning sun through the breaks of the Rio Puerco toward the towering black form of Cabezon butte.

The world looked and felt different to both of them. Something had changed inside them and they both knew they would never be the same again.

❖

CHAPTER II - THE KILLING GROUND

For over an hour Jed and Lucy walked silently. Neither felt a need for words, their feelings said it all. Every sight and sound and scent was enhanced and the world was beautiful and they were alive.

As they entered a small grove of Cottonwoods alongside a rare spring Jed broke the silence.

"Let's rest a bit Lucy. This sun takes its toll on us white boys."

Lucy smiled and sat down on the moist sand and leaned against an ancient Cottonwood. Jed plopped down and lay his head in her lap.

"You know Lucy," Jed began speaking slowly. "I saw you and felt you last night in a way that was totally new for me. You used the word love last night and it gave me a shiver then. And ever since I've had this very funny feeling."

"So are you saying I gave you a cold?"

"No. Of course not," Jed answered sitting up. "I'm saying that I think I'm in love with you."

Lucy closed her eyes and looked at the ground then sighed and smiled at Jed. "I'm afraid I love you too white boy."

Jed reached up and pulled Lucy to the ground and kissed her. As he held her close Jed looked at Lucy and said, "You are a very rare lady. I don't know anyone else who would have even wanted me around under the circumstances, much less wanted to make love."

Lucy pushed Jed off of her and said, "Did it bother you belagana? Do you think it was savage of me to want you inside of me last night while my sister lay dying."

"No . . . I . . . " Jed started to answer but Lucy continued.

"I wanted you because you make me feel alive and all around me there was death. Yes, its true that Indian people live closer to their death all the time and because of that we try to live life to the fullest all the time. Can you deal with that?"

"Oh yes. No problem. Believe me I have no complaints." Jed answered feeling thoroughly chastised.

There was silence for a while until Jed spoke again. "Lucy, if I'm out of line again just tell me and I"ll forget it . . . but I've been wondering . . . if you know why Rose and her baby were so sick."

"Of course I know why Jed," Lucy answered quickly. "Rose and her baby, and her two other babies by the way, died from the same thing that killed her husband Lawrence six months ago."

Jed looked puzzled. Lucy continued. "Thousands of Indian people have died from the same shameful cause."

Jed shook his head. "I'm sorry Lucy, I don't know what you're talking about."

Lucy sighed. "I'm talking about people from Laguna to Shiprock and Kayenta to Gallup who had the misfortune of living where the Goddamned Uranium companies decided to put their fucking mines and mills. Where have you been living Jed? This has been going on for 30 years. Oh don't tell me. Have the newspapers and TV in Santa Fe been too busy covering art shows and movie stars to cover this story?"

"Well . . ." Jed began slowly. "There have been a few stories over the years but I guess I just didn't realize . . ."

"Its all right Jed, you didn't make the mess and there's nothing you or anyone else can do about it. The poison ground in Indian country was made by the dominant culture. That's just the way they look at the land, and people who live close to the earth are just in the way. They've done it everywhere that anything that will produce revenue can be found. And they'll keep doing it until they kill each other out or burn up the planet."

"There must be some way to help," Jed said rubbing his head. "Some government agency must have responsibility for dealing with this sort of thing. Surely someone could help with this."

Lucy laughed. "Jed you're too far away from reality in your little archaeologist's world. First of all, the people who caused this problem are all from the big corporations that keep their politicians in government and secondly the people who are suffering are all Indians living way out there in remote sheep camps. Out of sight out of mind. Nobody cares, Jed, and they never will."

Lucy pointed to Mount Taylor off to the southwest and said, "All around that mountain, Jed, people are dying in the same way that Rose died. There are dozens of mines and mills all around that sacred mountain of the south. Have you ever seen the Ratbox Mine? Have you ever seen the Grubstake, Python and Aron McCall Mills? Rose lived over there in a canyon coming off the Mesa Montanosa, just downwind from Aron McCall's mill. She couldn't sweep often enough to keep the tailings out of her hogan. Lawrence worked for 6 years at the Gulf Mine. The companies and the government killed them just like they used to do with the cavalry. Its still genocide Jed, they just have different ways of carrying out the policy now."

Tears were running down Lucy's face as she spoke. Jed was also close to tears as he pulled Lucy to him and said, "I'm sorry darlin. I'm very sorry I've been so blind. I'm ashamed of what my race and culture has done to yours. I would like to see some of these places you told me about. Will you show me? Can we go see them together?"

Lucy stood back from Jed and asked, "Why would you want to see these things? What good would it do?"

"I want to see if something can be done about it," Jed answered. "I want to be able to describe the problems from first hand experience. I live in Santa Fe and know a lot of people in government agencies. Surely some public health or land management agency can do something if only they understand the problems."

"Jed, you're a hopeless crusader," Lucy said holding him by the shoulders. "Don't you know that millions of dollars have been spent by white people trying to figure out how to clean up this mess and nothing has ever changed. Babies keep dying and the wind keeps blowing this nuclear garbage over more of Indian country every day."

"Please understand," Jed pleaded. "I have to try. Will you show me some of the places you talked about?"

Lucy turned her back on Jed for several minutes and buried her head in her hands. "All right," she finally said. "I'll show you what the white men have done to Tsoodzix besides change its name to Mount Taylor, but we're gonna do it on Indian ponies. Ok?"

"Sure," Jed answered. "Why not?"

Lucy laughed and said, "We better eat. You're gonna need your strength if you're gonna ride with me for two or three days and keep me happy at night too."

They ate their meal of carne seca and water in the cool shade of the old Cottonwoods as Lucy described the route they would take around the sacred mountain. They were happy in the way that only lovers can be and they chased each other like children all the way back to the hogan.

The mid afternoon sun was brilliant and it bleached much of the color and contrast from the landscape. It took Lucy's sharp eyes to locate her grandmother's pony herd grazing on a hillside about a half mile away. Lucy only smiled when Jed offered to catch the three horses they would need for their journey.

By the time Jed returned sweaty and dust covered and without a single horse Lucy had nearly completed packing the panniers with the gear they would need.

"Lucy!" Jed announced panting as he pulled cactus spines from his boots.

"Those horses are wild. I don't think we'll be able to catch them. And I don't think they could be ridden or packed anyway."

"Ummm . . . that's too bad," Lucy said sounding concerned as she filled an empty coffee can with dry corn. She walked a few steps away from the grain shed and sounded the shrill tremolo that only Indian women seem to know how to make while shaking the corn in the coffee can.

In less than a minute all the horses came running to Lucy muzzling her gently like overgrown pet dogs.

Jed looked a little embarrassed as he asked, "Is there anything I can do to help."

"Sure," Lucy answered. "Saddle that bay and that roan . . . if you think you can handle it."

Jed only grunted in response as he haltered the two horses Lucy had pointed out. By the time he cinched down the last of them Lucy had the pack saddle on a gray mare and was ready to hang the loaded panniers.

"Help me out here mister," she ordered and Jed complied.

By the time all was ready it was nearly two o'clock and Lucy told Jed they would have to push hard to reach her chosen campsite on Mesa Chivato before dark. The two did ride hard all afternoon and into the early evening before climbing the steep and narrow trail up the mesa to a stock tank and windmill not far from the lava escarpment that capped this flat forested highland.

The horses were unloaded by moonlight and were fed and watered before Jed and Lucy thought of their own needs. Dinner was simple and quiet and afterward as Jed cleaned up the dishes in a basin of tepid water from the stock tank he began to hatch another idea.

"You know . . . this water is downright warm," he said looking over at Lucy lying on the saddle blankets. "And I could sure use a bath."

"Yes you sure could Jed. Why don't you do that?"

"Well . . . " Jed continued. "The only problem with that is I'd feel real lonely in this big tank all alone. And I wouldn't be able to reach all the places that need washing."

Lucy raised herself up on her elbows and looked over toward Jed standing and smiling in the moonlight. "Do you need help honey?" she asked with mock concern.

"Yes." Jed answered sounding as helpless as he could.

Lucy stood up, walked slowly over to Jed and looked at him for a minute without speaking. "Well how are you going to take a bath with your clothes on?" she asked tossing back her thick hair.

"Good point," Jed answered as he proceeded to disrobe.

Jed stepped into the 3 feet or so of tepid water in the big steel tank then sat down and immersed himself. When Jed emerged from the water he watched Lucy climbing in with a bottle of Dr. Bronners soap and a sponge. The two washed each other with a passion and interest that continued long after they left the tank. They slept well under a starry canopy that night waking only a few times to reaffirm their passion.

The next morning was brilliant as only a New Mexico morning can be. Jed and Lucy started out in the cool morning air heading southward along an old trail that followed the rim rock of Chivato Mesa. Off to the southwest the high ridges of the San Mateo Mountains rose from the top of the mesa. At the south end of the high country were the snow covered peaks of Tsoodzix, sacred mountain of the south to the Diñe, or Navajo, as the Spanish called them.

The highest of these peaks was called Mount Taylor by the whites. These are volcanic highlands reaching 11,000 feet with a violent history in the recent past. The last great lava flow from this mountain was called El Malpais by the Spanish Conquistadors.

This huge basaltic lava flow occurred less than 2000 years ago in a time when the area was heavily populated by the mysterious Anasazi. These ancient North Americans built large towns and road networks all over the four corners region.

Jed was well acquainted with Anasazi culture. He had been a contract archaeologist in the region for almost 20 years. He had been among the first to recognize and document the extensive Chaco road system, and he had located dozens of un-excavated Chacoan outlier towns. In spite of his often frazzled appearance, Jed was widely regarded as an expert on the architecture and ceramics of the Anasazi. His work had been published a number of times and because of his reputation he was able to make a fair and steady income in a field that is often characterized by starving professionals.

Jed had heard an old legend re-told many times in the modern Rio Grande Pueblos of how Tsoodzix had been caused to erupt by the caciques or high priests of Chaco Canyon to the north of Tsoodzix. According to the story another great city once existed under El Malpais but the inhabitants had grown wicked and had lost the path. They had become slave traders and dealers in all manner of evil.

To put an end to this evil, so the story goes, the caciques at Chaco used their power to influence the forces of nature and caused a great lava flow to cover the city. This was one of a thousand legends Jed had heard over the years and he had paid it very little heed as his primary interests in the Anasazi were ceramic arts and building styles. The significance of this old story was soon to increase for Jed though he did not know it yet.

As Jed rode along the rim rock that morning his thoughts were all of beauty. The beauty of the spectacular scenery all around him and the beauty of the woman who rode in front of him. At that point Jed was as happy as he could ever remember being.

After a long morning of silence and smiles Lucy turned to Jed and spoke, "We're gonna start dropping off the mesa soon. The trail is very steep and narrow. Keep an eye on the panniers and let me know if they're gonna hit a rock or anything."

"Will do, patrona," Jed answered with a grin.

Soon enough they did begin a precipitous decent through boulder fields and over rock ledges. At several spots Jed shouted to Lucy that it looked like the panniers would not fit between rocks but each time Lucy carefully led the old pack mare safely through.

About half way down the mesa they emerged onto a wide geologic bench covered with range grasses and stunted junipers. From that open vantage point they had a clear view of the Ratbox Uranium Mine, largest open pit uranium mine in the world.

"Jesus Christ!" Jed shouted. "What the fuck is that?"

"That's the Ratbox," Lucy answered. "And that's what's left of the Laguna village of Paguate," she continued, pointing to a pitiful cluster of adobe buildings perched on the edge of the highwall. Jed could see bright blue pools of water in the pit below the highwall and a small stream connecting them that flowed into a large reservoir in the distance.

"What's in that water?" he asked assuming that Lucy would have an answer.

"Only God and the EPA know for sure," Lucy answered grimly. "But I've heard things like radium, cobalt, uranium, and cadmium are there in ample quantities."

"Do any people use that water?" Jed asked looking at the distant reservoir.

"Only Indians and their livestock," Lucy replied as she prodded her horse back onto the narrow trail.

Jed and Lucy were as silent as the hills as they descended the rest of the mesa escarpment and rode through the half dead village of Paguate. The few people who were outside did not acknowledge their presence. They turned their faces away from the strangers on horseback as if in shame. The remnant population of Paguate seemed as shattered, broken, and hopeless as their homes clinging to the edge of the poisonous pit.

The desperation these people felt now was a far cry from the dominant state of mind during the heyday of mining. Throughout the decade of the seventies the Laguna people were the most prosperous of the Pueblo Indians.

They were partners with the giant mining conglomerate, Python. Everyone had a good job, there were plenty of new pick up trucks and everybody was happy.

Then the ore began to play out. At first it was just a few layoffs, then a few more until finally one day Python was gone and nothing was left except the devastation.

Depression and despair followed hard on the heels of Python's departure. Now in the eighties the Laguna people had the dubious distinction of having the highest suicide rate of any tribe in America.

The dream had passed, the lie had ended. Now where sheep had once grazed there was a giant poisonous trench. The people who once lived happily in egalitarian poverty now had no way to live. The Lagunas that did not kill themselves were either drinking themselves to death or dying of one or more common varieties of cancer induced by their proximity to the Ratbox.

Jed and Lucy rode silently through Paguate, around the west end of the Ratbox pit across the trickle of the Rio Moquino and back into the dry foot hills of the San Mateos.

By the time they reached the rim rock again the sun had dropped below the western horizon and the entire sky was ablaze with color. Lucy led them into a dirt tank with a small log corral beside it. By the time they finished caring for the horses it was dark again.

After a simple dinner the cool of the evening and other natural motivations drove the two lovers to seek the warmth of wool blankets and each other. In the tingling afterglow of lovemaking they lay silently looking at the stars as meteors streaked by.

Jed finally broke the silence. "I'm so lucky," he said turning his head toward Lucy. "My life is so good. I have everything I need. I have you to hold. I'm healthy. I'm free. And so many others have none of these things. I want to do something for those people in Paguate. I want to help people like your sister Rose. I owe it to the universe for making my life so good and easy."

"That's great Jed," Lucy answered still looking at the stars. "But don't let it possess you. There's only so much one person can do. I'm glad you care. That's part of why I love you. I just don't want to lose you to a hopeless cause."

"I've got to try to do something about this God awful mess, Lucy. I know if this was happening outside of Santa Fe it wouldn't be tolerated. I'm going to do something about it one way or another. And don't worry about me, I can handle it."

"Can you handle this again?" Lucy asked smiling as she crawled on top of Jed.

"Indeed I can," Jed answered.

And indeed he did. And sleep was sound after love was sweet.

The next day was full of steep and rocky trails, biting flies, sweat, and rattlesnakes. By the time they had crossed the ridge below Tsoodzix and entered Rinconada Canyon Jed felt completely used up. It was only noon as they watered the horses in Rinconada Creek and already Jed was thinking they should make camp.

"Don't you think this would be a nice place to stay tonight?" Jed asked hoping Lucy would agree.

"Well Jed," Lucy answered with a sigh. "My granny tried to warn me about belagana boys. Yea, she told me you were all weak and were only interested in lying around copulating. I guess she was right."

Jed stood up quickly from where he had been lying beside the creek. "Hey, I'm fine. I could ride like this for a week and not even think of copulating. Let's go."

Lucy nearly choked trying to contain her laughter as she mounted up and led the pack mare across the creek. Jed soaked his old felt hat in the creek pulled it tightly on his head and followed Lucy without another word.

Lucy made her way to an eroded old roadbed that led to an abandoned coal strip mine on the ridge between Rinconada and Guadalupe Canyons.

"What is this?" Jed asked as they rode onto the ugly gash of the strip mine.

"It's an old coal mine Python operated in the early 50's so they could run the boilers in their uranium mill at Bluewater. My Grandpa used to work up here. He told me all about it," Lucy answered.

Lucy and Jed rode along this slash in the landscape for over a mile before they got back onto a regular trail again. They followed this steep and narrow trail up and over the next ridge through a heavy stand of Ponderosa and White Fir and into a large sloping meadow that overlooked the uranium boomtown of Grants. When Jed saw this dusty extension of civilization he got an idea that would not go away.

"Hey Lucy," he called out after perfecting his idea for a few moments. "Let's go down there to Grants and stay in a motel tonight."

"What?" Lucy asked in disbelief. "You want to ride out of these mountains and go into that filthy little town and spend money to stay in a cheap Route 66 motel?"

"Yea," Jed answered with a cocky smile. "I sure do."

"Well," Lucy said slowly. "You do need a bath, and I would like to eat something besides carne seca and tortillas. But what are we gonna do with the horses?"

"We'll work it out when we get there," Jed answered. "Let's just get down there and get in a shower together and roll around between some real sheets for a change."

Lucy looked thoughtful for a minute then said, "Good idea belagana. But don't forget food. And don't forget that we have to make sure my Grandma's horses are safe."

Jed smiled his assurance to Lucy and the two began to pick their way down from the mountain to the uranium capitol of the world.

This once busy mining boom town looked dead as they approached old Route 66. All of the buildings, roads, signs, even the dogs seemed tired and used up. Even when this modern boom town was growing like a cancer it wasn't very appealing. But then aesthetics were never the point.

Like all the mining boom towns of the American west, Grants was intended to serve the basic visceral needs of the miners. Shelter, drink, food, and whores, none in outstanding quality but in sufficient quantity to mollify the hard laboring masses. And that was enough as long as the ore was good and the market high.

Now the glory days were some years passed and the dust and decay was setting in. Those that hung on in the desperate hope that the good days would come again were few in number and poor in both spirit and pocketbook.

Most of the old Route 66 motels and restaurants were built in the 40's and 50's and had long since slipped past their prime. Some of them were absolute dumps while a few were maintained just enough to stay out of trouble with the health department. All of them engaged in a constant contest to see who could afford the lowest room rates and still remain in business.

The Atomic Motel and Cafe looked as though it had seen healthier days as Jed and Lucy rode up to the office. The sporadically flashing neon atom above the office door was glowing in only two of its three electron orbits. The third elliptical neon tube was broken near the top by what appeared to be a .44 caliber bullet hole.

Lucy held the horses as Jed stepped into the motel office. There was no one in the motel office when Jed entered. He walked up to the trash covered desk and rang the service bell. There was no response. Jed could hear a TV playing behind a ratty curtain that separated the office from the manager's house. After a few minutes of waiting Jed stepped behind the desk and peered cautiously behind the curtain.

There, sitting in a junkyard easy chair with a nearly empty bottle of Jim Beam whiskey in hand, was an ancient old man. The old man appeared to be asleep even though he was sitting upright and the TV was blaring Mighty Mouse cartoons less than two feet from him.

"Excuse me," Jed said politely. "I'd like a room."

There was no response so Jed spoke louder.

"Hey . . . I want to rent a room." Still there was no response.

The thought entered Jed's mind that the old man might be dead. He slowly walked into the room but before he was halfway to the old man a dog in the next room began to bark. The old man opened his eyes and stood up still clutching the whiskey bottle in his left hand and brandishing a .45 caliber Colt in the other.

"Who the hell are you?" The old man wheezed as he pointed the antique revolver at Jed.

"Jesus Christ . . . I'm a customer," Jed answered backing away quickly.

"A customer?" The old man repeated as though he had forgotten the meaning of the term.

"Yes," Jed assured him. "A customer. I want a room for me and my lady. And I need a safe place to picket my horses for the night."

The old man wrinkled up his already corrugated face and looked hard at Jed through what appeared to be his only good eye.

"Horses . . . you say you want a safe place to keep your horses around here?"

"Right," Jed answered. "Three of them."

The old man rubbed the tobacco stained stubble on his chin and looked hard at Jed again.

"Hell son," he said as he spit on the floor. "There ain't no safe place for nuthin' in this town no more. All the good folks is gone. There ain't none here now but mighty bad folks. Drugs and fornication and theivin'. That's all folks round here do nowadays. No sir them horses'd be stole for sure and probably a fornicated by folks on drugs. I don't think I can help you son."

"Well," Jed said with a sigh. "Thank you just the same."

Jed was out the door and just about to tell Lucy the sad news when the old man stepped outside and said, "Wait a minute son. Maybe I can help you after all. I don't have any customers right now and I can put you and your woman there up in my nicest room. And if you'll give me a hand moving out the beds your horses can have a room of their own."

The old man spit and smiled broadly as if to verify the sincerity of his offer. Lucy looked back at the mountains above town shaking her head and muttering in Navajo.

Jed looked at Lucy, then at the old man, then laughed and said, "You got a deal old timer. Let's move the beds."

The old man grinned, finished off his whisky, threw the bottle over his shoulder and motioned for Jed to follow him. He and Jed quickly emptied a room of its sparse furnishings and covered the floor with straw from a shed behind the motel. Jed filled the bath tub with water and put fresh hay and grain in one corner of the room.

Jed and Lucy removed the horses tack and brushed them down then turned them into their accommodations for the night. They seemed satisfied with the services and soon settled in to eating and drinking.

Jed paid for the horses and humans and got the key to he and Lucy's room. When they were finally alone in the room Lucy began to laugh and said, "I don't understand how you crazy belaganas managed to take over the world. I've never seen anything as dumb as putting horses in a motel room."

"Well, now, Lucy," Jed answered in his fake drawl. "You just don't understand. There are drug crazed horse fornicators in these parts. And I'm just trying to protect your granny's horses from them."

"Horse fornicators?" Lucy asked looking sick.

"Right," Jed answered with certainty. "The old man warned me about them."

"Uh huh . . . well my granny did try to warn me . . . but its too late now. But listen Jed," Lucy continued pointing to the wall above the bed. "Before you get any ideas about fornication, that velvet nude of Dolly Parton has to go."

"Really?" Jed asked looking sideways at the picture. "I think it has considerable artistic merit."

"Well if you believe that," Lucy answered quickly. "You can move in with the horses right now."

Jed grabbed Lucy and they both rolled onto the bed laughing. In spite of the dilapidated surroundings they both had a grand time in the shower and in the squeaky bed and they slept in their junkyard suite until the sun was high above Mount Taylor the next morning. Before leaving town they enjoyed a hot breakfast of huevos rancheros at the Uranium Cafe on Main Street.

Jed and Lucy rode though an empty city park beside the Chamber of Commerce and past empty houses on a short dusty street that ended at the base of the mesa above town. Lucy led them up another steep and twisting trail that eventually broke through the rimrock and led them west across the flat mesa top.

From the west edge of the mesa they had a commanding view of the plain that stretched from the forested Zuni Mountains in the south to Mesa Montanosa in the north.

Two out of place seeming industrial facilities with adjacent enormous piles of sand dominated the otherwise nearly empty plain. Great plumes of dust trailed off the sand piles in the prevailing west winds. Lucy pointed to the dust plumes and said, "There lie two of the biggest piles of rat poison in the world."

"Rat poison?" Jed asked making a pained face.

"Uranium mill tailings actually," Lucy answered. "The biggest piles of that kind of shit in the world. And it probably would kill rats. It sure has killed some people, including my sister and her family."

Jed's chin dropped to his chest.

"Did Rose live down there somewhere?"

"Actually she lived over there," Lucy answered pointing toward Mesa Montanosa. "On the other side of the mesa in Red Rock Canyon. Just downwind from the Aron McCall mill tailings. You'll see later on. Come on let's go."

Jed followed along silently behind Lucy thinking about the enormous wrong that had been done to the land below him. He remembered not long ago reading a story about how badly polluted the wells were in this part of New Mexico because of the mines and the mill tailings. He felt ashamed at how quickly he had forgotten that story until now when someone he knew and loved had been hurt by that deadly pollution.

"White people are too damn comfortable," he thought.

People in Santa Fe, he concluded, are so wrapped up in their art and culture and coolness that they're blinded to the wretched conditions Indian people are living and dying in just 200 miles away. He knew this well because for years he was a master practitioner in the art of cool comfortable Santa Fe living. He was in fact more guilty than most since his work as an archaeologist took him into Indian country frequently. He had somehow blocked out the scenes that weren't pleasing and lived only for bones, broken pottery, and ancient masonry.

Now that his life was bound up with someone who lived this reality he was finally awake and aware of the truth, and he did not like what he saw. Jed had drifted deep into his guilt and concentration and much of the day had passed by without his notice when suddenly Lucy's voice brought him back to the world.

"That's Ambrosia Lake," she said waving her hand at a huge basin north of Mesa Montanosa. "And that's the Aron McCall Mill," She continued pointing in the direction of another industrial complex with its companion tailings pile.

"Where is Rose's place?" Jed asked.

"There in the mouth of that little canyon just this side of the mill," Lucy answered wiping her eyes.

Even from this distance Jed could see a beautiful little blue roofed hogan with a few out buildings and small pens and corrals. He thought of the hopes and dreams and love that once filled those spaces and how it had all been lost to greed. Jed wondered how any group of men could ever be allowed to destroy homes and families for the sake of money. And now that it had obviously happened, Jed was even more puzzled at why nothing was being done to clean up the deadly mess left in the wake of the pillage.

That evening Jed was still deep in thought as he and Lucy ate beside a small campfire. Lucy was able to coax him back into the physical world for an hour or so, but as he lay there beneath the stars again afterward, he once again found himself pondering the great question of why. Without much change in thought pattern he slipped under sleep's veil and spent an uneasy night dreaming of nuclear bombs and erupting volcanoes.

As Lucy and Jed rode north along Mesa Chivato the next morning the surreal view into Ambrosia Lake with its forests of mine headframes and giant tailings piles faded behind them. It was replaced by the endless desert plain of the San Juan Basin.

The rolling vastness of the brown hills below them was scarcely broken by the few scattered junipers along arroyos. There were a few mysterious groves of cottonwoods that looked like islands in the sea. These rare oases were extremely valuable to a host of area wildlife and had been venerated by Navajos and other resident aboriginals for thousands of years.

As they progressed northward another great black anomaly began to appear on the plain. It was the Bee Ranch coal mine with its giant shovels extracting fossil solar energy and killing the springs that supported the lush and mysterious groves of cottonwoods.

Jed was more troubled than ever about the massive destruction that was going on all around Tsoodzix. He felt the need to talk about it so he trotted up beside Lucy.

"Why is it?" he asked. "That this particular part of the earth was so heavily mined?"

Lucy said nothing for a few moments then looked over at Jed and answered, "You know Jed . . . there's probably a lot of places around with just as much coal and uranium as here. But most other places have a problem that gets in the way of tearing up the land and poisoning the water."

"What's that?" Jed asked looking puzzled.

"White folks," Lucy answered with a knowing smile. "Yea . . . white folks," she repeated. "You know Jed I wouldn't be surprised to find out that Santa Fe was sitting on top of tons of uranium and coal and shit. But the mess it would make getting it out of the ground just wouldn't go well with pink coyotes."

Lucy trotted on ahead pulling the pack mare with her and leaving Jed in a billowing cloud of dust. As Jed tried to hold his breath until the dust settled he thought that in spite of her joking tone Lucy was probably right.

By mid afternoon Jed and Lucy were back to their first night's campsite eating lunch and looking north to Cabezon. Jed was chewing thoughtfully on a red chile covered piece of carne seca.

He looked at the metal tank with fond memories then looked at Lucy and said, "How about a bath, sweetheart?"

Lucy shook her head and raised her arms as if addressing an audience. "Granny you were right!" she shouted toward Cabezon. "All these belaganas want to do is fornicate. Nothing more!"

Lucy turned back to Jed and spoke like a parent scolding a child.

"Jed you know if we get naked now in the middle of the day we won't leave this place till tomorrow. And there in the distance I can see the smoke of my Granny's woodstove. She's probably cooking beans and rice with whole chiles and I want some tonight. And then I want to crawl between the blankets with you and use your body. Ok?"

"Let's get with it." Jed said as he swung on to his horse.

Lucy was smiling as she led her horses on to the steep trail down the Chivato escarpment.

When they reached the base of the mesa the horses seemed to sense the end of the long ride and though tired and dust covered they quickened their pace. By the time they reached Lucy's Grandmother's place it was nearly dark. The crimson band that colored the western horizon was fading and was being replaced by a clear star filled evening.

Jed and Lucy cared for the horses and stored away the tack in the silent darkness. Coyotes were singing love songs in the distance as the silver moon rose above the Nacimientos. Jed and Lucy washed up at the windmill, did indeed eat beans and rice with whole red chiles, and spent their last night together for a while in the bed of Jed's pick up.

The creaking leaf springs of the truck harmonized with the coyotes as the two lovers made the most of their last hours together. Jed's dreams were full of mixed passion from the new level of love he felt for Lucy and for his quest to find a way to heal the ravaged lands he had witnessed on the ride.

The killing ground he had seen all around the great mountain left indelible images in Jed's mind. The passion and the vision quest that those images had sparked would change his life in ways he could not even imagine. The long ride with Lucy around Tsoodzix was simply the first step in a great journey that would take him to the known limits of the human mind and then would force him into that great unknown wilderness beyond the limits.

❖

CHAPTER III - HOME TO SANTA FE

After a lingering and somewhat tearful goodbye Jed finally rolled back down the dusty track toward Torreon. By shortly after noon he pulled back on to the pavement near Hostene George's place. He did not stop for chile mutton stew.

Jed did pick up a burrito and a beer in Cuba before heading up highway 126 toward the crest of the Nacimientos. Beyond the crest the road became a two rut Forest Service track that was often quite muddy from snow melt, and rutted from an over abundance of log trucks. Jed slithered back onto pavement at Fenton Lake and drove his mud covered rig to the parking area across the Jemez River from the Spence Hot Springs.

Jed smiled as he walked across the log bridge over the river. He remembered wild nights 20 years earlier when hordes of naked people too stoned to remember their names would attempt this crossing and often ended up thrashing in the river.

The springs were almost empty this weekday afternoon. There were only two young women in the middle pool. They both said hello as Jed undressed at the edge of the pool. Jed nodded in response as he dropped his shirt to the ground and stepped into the first truly hot water his body had felt for nearly a week.

As usual the springs felt wonderful and Jed positioned himself in a rocky corner and closed his eyes to savor the feeling. In a few minutes Jed heard rustling in the water and then felt the brush of a hand against his leg. He opened his eyes and saw that the two women were sitting on either side of him. They smiled and he smiled back.

"We're both students at the New Age School of Massage Therapy in Santa Fe." one of them announced." And we wondered if we could practice on you."

Jed shook his head and looked skyward. "Well ... " He answered slowly. "I'd have to be a fool to say no." The two students worked Jed over from head to toe and they were indeed skilled in their chosen trade. Jed felt like a jellyfish trying to dress himself as the two women watched smiling some two hours later.

"Maybe we'll see you in Santa Fe sometime." one of them said as Jed stumbled away from the pool.

"Maybe," Jed answered with a wave as he disappeared into the forest.

"Thank you grandfather creator for giving me this wonderful life," Jed whispered to the trees and sky as he made his way back to his truck.

Evening caught up with Jed before he made it back home. The lights of Santa Fe looked very good to him as he topped the hill north of town.

When Jed got home there were more than a dozen notes tacked to his front door from friends and part time lovers. His mailbox was stuffed with bills and letters. Most of the letters appeared to be from agencies and individuals he owed archaeological reports to.

Jed was back in the white man's world and he was not quite ready for it. He poured himself a stiff drink of Jack Daniels and rolled a joint and sat down on his well worn Taos couch to think.

The booze and dope did not clear the images of the past week from his head but they did convince him that it was time to sleep. He would deal with the white world and what the white world had done to the Indian world tomorrow.

Jed was awakened from his troubled sleep by the strangely unfamiliar sound of his telephone ringing. He stumbled half asleep and naked through the hallway and into the living room. He picked up the phone and answered in a tired voice. "What?"

An angry voice responded, "Is that you Jed Flyway?"

Jed recognized the voice as that of a Forest Service contracting agent who no doubt wanted an archaeological report that was overdue before Jed left for his visit with Lucy. Suddenly Jed was wide awake and began to lie rapidly.

"Listen Alex, I know you need the report so you can submit your grant application. I have the completed report right here in front of me."

There was nothing in front of Jed except the petrified remains of a pizza he had ordered several weeks before.

"I have to send that report in by Friday," the caller continued in only a slightly calmer voice. "That's the deadline for applications for this year's trail crew grant. Without your report and clearances there will be no trail work in the Carson this summer. And if that happens Jed you will never work for the Forest Service again."

"Relax Alex," Jed assured him in a calm voice. "I have the completed report right here, and it was packaged and ready to send to you a week ago. There must've been some mix up with my secretary."

Jed had no secretary but the assurances seemed to help since Alex began to talk in his normal federal bureaucrat's voice.

As he continued his rambling dialogue there was a knock on Jed's front door. Without thinking about his state of total undress Jed stood up carrying the phone and opened the door.

The young woman standing at the door with her Afghan hound seemed not at all shocked by Jed's nudity. She was in fact obviously pleased to see him. She hugged him tightly and kissed him as her dog jumped around excitedly peeing in little squirts.

Jed was still trying to respond to his caller as all this occurred.

Finally in an attempt to gain control of the situation Jed said, "Listen Alex. Someone is here, I've got to go."

Then he quickly hung up the phone and turned his attention to the red haired woman clinging to him.

"Christie!" Jed shouted at the woman. "Will you control this damn dog? Its peeing on everything."

Christie puckered her lips and began to talk like an infant. "Oh Jed she's just happy to see you like me. Isn't she a sweetie?"

"No!" Jed answered. "She isn't. She's a dog and she's making a mess in my hoooooouuuuuu . . . shit she just licked my balls. You and the dog need to go. I have a lot to do."

It was then that Jed realized that an elderly couple out for their morning stroll and two joggers had stopped on the street and were enjoying the entertainment at his doorway.

He grabbed Christie and pulled her inside and slammed the door. "Just a minute," Jed said as he quickly grabbed a bathrobe. "Now listen Christie," he began holding up a finger in her face.

"No Jed you listen," she interrupted. "I've been trying to get in touch with you for over a week. No one knew where you were. Michael Bogan is having an opening tonight at the Perez Gallery and I want you to go with me. Everyone will be there. You know I hear Robert Redford's place up in Rancho Encantado is full of Bogan pieces. I just have to be there with you tonight Jed so you can interpret all the symbolism of Bogan's art. He is so wonderful Jed. I know you'll love it, he researches all the works so carefully. I understand he actually lived in Moencopi for a week before painting his corn maiden." Please say you'll go with me Jed . . . pleeeeaaase." She finished her long winded appeal by rubbing the inside of Jed's thigh. Jed pushed her hand away and stepped back.

"No!" he answered with a tone of absolute assurance. "I can't go. And I don't want to go. I'm very busy on a project. Ok? Now its very good to see you . . . and your dog . . . but I'm busy and you have to go now."

Christie took a deep breath and looked sideways at Jed. "You know Jed," she purred. "I can remember times when you didn't care what you were doing . . . you would stop anything for an hour or two with me."

Jed looked dejected. He knew this was true. He had been an enthusiastic part time lover with Christie for over five years.

She had ventured to Santa Fe from southern California after reading *Book of the Hopi* and *Monkey Wrench Gang*. She came with a seemingly un-limited trust fund and an un-quenchable thirst for wildness.

She had slaked her thirst at the well of northern New Mexico and had become drunk from it. Jed was one of a dozen or more men who met her criteria for wildness. It was said that she and a wild eyed young writer from Taos had managed the act of copulation at over 90 miles per hour on a motorcycle screaming through the Rio Grande Gorge at three in the morning. As Jed looked at her and thought of these things he shook his head in disbelief at some of the things she had talked him into. He touched her on the shoulder and said, "Christie . . . I have had one hell of a good time with you and I regret nothing. But I have to tell you many things are happening in my life. Things that I never expected. I am finding a new meaning for my existence and I am driven by a quest unlike anything I have ever felt. I'm sorry, Christie, but I don't think I would fit in your life any more. But I'm sure you'll have no trouble finding someone who does."

Christie tossed her thick red hair back and looked at Jed and sighed. "Oh well Jed Flyway. If you've decided to grow old or fall in love or something like that then there's nothing I can do about it. And yes I'm sure I'll find someone to go with tonight. But remember, when your new life becomes too tame and your lover becomes dull, I'll be around. I'll still be finding new ways to get off. Look me up if you don't grow fat and useless."

Jed nodded and let her and her dog out of the door. He watched her picture perfect ass slither through the garden gate and for a moment he wondered if he really had changed.

Jed looked up at a cloud drifting above Santa Fe Baldy and remembered Lucy and what they had shared in the past week and his moment of weakness passed. He went inside and fixed himself a breakfast burrito and began to think of anyone he knew in the government who might help with the radioactive legacy in Indian country.

Jed spent most of the day putting together something that would suffice as his overdue report for the Forest Service. As he organized and typed his field notes he continued to think of who in the government might be able to help get the uranium mess cleaned up.

Jed managed to put together a document by Friday that met all the basic requirements of his contract and he sent it off to the nervous administrator by Federal Express. He needed the final payment for this contract to finance what he envisioned would be his major effort at lobbying the appropriate agencies to eliminate the health risks in the uranium belt.

Jed was on the Plaza by 10:00 Saturday morning talking to old friends about his plans and asking for any suggestions of who to talk to. Four hours and six margaritas later Jed had a small list of mostly state bureaucrats who might have some jurisdiction over the issues he was interested in.

Jed spent most of the following Monday setting up appointments with the administrators of public health, environmental, and mine reclamation programs.

His first appointment was with Paul Earlick, the Bureau Chief of the Radiation Protection Bureau. Jed was at the Capitol South office complex by 9:00 AM Wednesday morning for his meeting with Mr. Earlick. Jed entered the domain of state bureaucracy with great confidence that he was about to initiate the solution of one of the worlds great environmental problems.

Jed smiled at the pretty young Spanish secretary and announced his purpose for being there. She smiled back through heavy make-up and offered him a cup of coffee and a comfortable seat on a Taos couch.

After a short and fashionable wait Jed was approached by a well dressed young man who greeted him with a distinctive Ivy League accent.

"Mr. Flyway? Yes, so good to meet you. I've heard such wonderful things about you. Won't you come in to my office. Yolanda please bring in the coffee and fill Mr. Flyway's cup."

Jed followed the well bred bureaucrat into a tastefully decorated office resplendently decorated with R.C. Gorman prints and Santa Clara pottery.

"Well," Mr. Earlick began flashing a toothy smile. "What can I do for you today Mr. Flyway?"

Jed propped his left boot up on to his right knee and began to speak slowly.

"Mr. Earlick, I just spent a week out in the Navajo checkerboard lands around Mt. Taylor and I became aware of the very serious health threat in that area due to all the uranium mines and mills. I witnessed the death of my girlfriend's sister from cancer caused by that mess. This young Navajo mother was one of many people who have died as a direct result of living in the middle of this radioactive garbage. I want to know what is being done and what can be done to clean up the land out there. I'm sure you'll agree that no one should be threatened in this way in their homes. I'm sure something can and will be done to eliminate this pox on the land.

I want to know if there's anything that a citizen like me can do to speed up the process. I can write editorials, I can write my congressman, anything you believe might be helpful. Anything."

Mr. Earlick was quiet for what seemed a long time. Finally he sighed deeply, folded his hands on his desk and began to speak rather softly.

"Yes. . . yes, indeed, Mr. Flyway . . . we are acutely aware of the health problems in the uranium belt. We have been monitoring that situation for many years. We know that there is serious contamination of groundwater and the air is tainted with radon and other particulates. We have entire rooms full of files on this very serious health and environmental problem. We have full time investigators compiling more data even as we speak. We know for certain that the problems in that area are not improving since the mining boom ended. They are in fact worsening and spreading. I have just this week asked the legislature for more funding to expand our aerial reconnaissance and hopefully broaden our baseline data regarding this problem."

Mr. Earlick smiled to indicate that he was through explaining the extent of his knowledge in this area.

Jed looked at him for a moment then said, "Yes well that's all fine . . . but what are you doing to eliminate the problems?"

Mr. Earlick looked away from Jed and through the window then straightened his tie and answered,

"Mr. Flyway. . . I. . . er. . . that is this bureau has no authority or funding to do anything but monitor the situation . . . and gather data."

"Well all right then," Jed said still hopeful for some solution. "Who is acting on your information and doing something?"

Mr. Earlick looked back out of the window then turned back to Jed and answered solemnly, "At present Mr. Flyway no agency is doing any reclamation work on the mill tailings and no one knows what to do about the groundwater."

Jed could not believe what he was hearing. He stared dumbfounded at Mr. Earlick for a few moments, then asked, "Who else is working in this area? Who can I talk to about this? There has to be someone somewhere with the authority and the funding to deal with this issue."

Mr. Earlick began to fidget and look at his watch.

"Mr. Flyway, there is a new federal uranium reclamation program that is just getting started. But I understand that the Grant's Uranium Belt is rather low on the list of priorities because of the lack of population."

"Lack of population!" Jed interrupted. "The death of one child should be enough to trigger a national response. What the hell does it take to be highly placed on the goddamned priority list."

Mr. Earlick was turning noticeably crimson as he answered.

"Please Mr. Flyway, many people feel as strongly as you about this situation but there is very little that can be done to change the federal criteria for listing these sites. The plain and simple fact is this, if an area has political clout they are more likely to receive funding for environmental cleanup work before an equally impacted area with less political influence. That's just how things work and I don't believe you or I can do anything to change that."

Jed looked quietly at the floor for a minute or more, then asked, "Who will be running this new program?"

Mr. Earlick straightened his tie and answered, "Well against my recommendation the state has given that program to a small agency called the Abandoned Mine Land Bureau. This is a poorly funded program that has had a degree of success in reclaiming some small problem mines around the state. The program director, however, is in my opinion a poor administrator and he clearly has a problem with authority figures and standard procedures. His name is Robert Simpson and his office is in the basement of the Villa Reina Building on Don Gaspar. If you really want to talk to Robert you can't miss his bureau. Just look for the offices that look like they've been ransacked and follow the loud rock music."

"All right," Jed said standing up and shaking hands with Mr. Earlick. "I think I will give it a try. And thanks for the . . . education."

Mr. Earlick smiled and showed Jed to the door.

As Jed stepped out into the bright light of mid morning he was beginning to see just how correct Lucy had been about the likelihood of finding a solution in the government for the poisoned legacy of weapons development. He decided he would give Robert Simpson a try and he took a chance on just walking in without an appointment.

Sure enough as Jed walked down the stairs into the basement of the Villa Reina Building he could hear the Grateful Dead playing "Cold Rain and Snow" at high volume. As he entered the offices of the Abandoned Mine Land Bureau it did indeed appear as though vandals had visited the place. There were maps and papers and books on the walls and floors and file cabinets. There were several small groups of people in T-shirts and jeans talking loudly to one another and paying no particular notice to Jed. A petite young woman was sitting at the desk nearest the entry talking rapidly in Spanish and painting her nails.

She noticed Jed and said, "You're looking for somebody . . . no?"

"Yes," Jed answered. "Robert Simpson."

"Eee . . . I think Bob is still in his office down there on the left . . . I mean right . . . Ok?"

She resumed her conversation and Jed followed her directions.

When Jed reached the indicated office door he saw a tall man with brown hair standing on a cluttered desk and looking intently at a USGS quadrangle. The walls were covered with similar maps and the chairs and desk were cluttered with a great variety of papers and publications.

Jed knocked on the open door to get the man's attention. The man turned and flashed a friendly smile and said, "Howdy, come on in." The tall man with bushy hair and full beard jumped down from the desk to greet Jed.

"Bob Simpson, what can I do for you?" he said holding out his hand.

"Jed Flyway. . . I'd like to talk to you about uranium if you've got a little time."

"Jed Flyway. . . hmmm," the man said stroking his beard. "You're an archaeologist aren't you?"

"Yea . . ." Jed answered. "I am that."

"Right," Bob Simpson continued. "I've heard a lot about you from the girls down at The Museum of New Mexico. They do most of my clearance work, and I dance a bit with some of them. From what I hear you've done a little dancin' with some of them too."

Both men smiled at each other in mutual understanding.

"Uh . . . yea," Jed said with a small chuckle. "I guess that's true. But you think we can talk a bit about the mines out around Mt. Taylor?"

"Sure, have a seat," Bob Simpson answered as he knocked a stack of books off a chair and sat on his desk with one boot propped up against the wall. Jed took a seat and began to explain his interest in uranium.

"You see Mr. Simpson," Jed began. "My girl friend is Navajo and I just got back from a very heavy week with her out around Mt. Taylor. Her sister and her newborn child died from the effects of living close to all the abandoned mines and mills around there. My girlfriend told me about all the other families that have been affected by this fucking uranium mess. I really had no idea it was so bad until we took a ride all the way around Mt. Taylor. I saw the Ratbox and some of the old mines and mill tailings on the other side of the mountain. I just couldn't believe that anything that bad could be done to land and people in the U.S. without some plan to clean it up. That's why I'm here today. I got your name from Paul Earlick. He told me about all the research that's being done on the health effects of all that shit but basically he said there were no plans to actually get started with any clean up activities. Is that true?"

Bob Simpson stomped his boot against the wall and took a deep breath. "Well first of all," he began. "Paul Earlick should be named Major Asslick.

He doesn't give a shit about anything but his image and his political future. But in this case I'm afraid he's right. I have managed to twist the rules and procedures and get a few small mines reclaimed to a point where its safe for now at least to live near them. But I have never had the funding that would be necessary to tackle the really big problems like the Ratbox or the big mill tailings. And I'm afraid I may never get that opportunity the way things are shaping up. Most of the money for the new uranium program is either going into straight research or to reclamation projects in Utah and Colorado where lots of white folks are screaming for a fix and their political pimps are getting their projects bumped up on the priority list. There's no question that taken collectively the uranium legacy in the Grants, Gallup, Shiprock belt is the largest and the worst in the country. The Ratbox alone would take billions to reclaim properly. It would cost many times more to fix the mess than any corporation derived in profit from making the mess. And I'm afraid, my friend, the will to spend that sort of money to protect Indians will never develop in Washington."

"Could it be cleaned up if the money were there?" Jed asked.

"Hell, we built the Panama Canal, we put people on the moon for Christsakes, if we had the collective will as a people we could certainly find the money and decency to wipe our asses when we shit on a piece of the earth. But partner . . . there aren't enough people like you. The best we can hope for is to learn a lesson from this mistake. If industry can't afford to restore the land then we can't afford to let them rip it up for short term profit for a few people."

Jed was stunned by what he had heard. He sat silently with his chin in his hand.

Bob Simpson scratched his beard and said, "Listen I know I haven't been much help but I'm trying to tell you the truth. There is no government quick fix for this mess. But I'll tell you what . . . I can offer you a birds eye view of the mess around Mt. Taylor if that would help you understand the magnitude of the problem."

Jed lifted his eyes and asked, "What do you mean?"

"I've got four hours scheduled on the state helicopter for site reconnaissance this week. And today is a beautiful day for flying. We could cover the whole Mt. Taylor district and be back in a couple of hours. You're welcome to come along if you like."

Jed thought for a moment then answered, "Sure that would be great . . . if it wont get you in any trouble."

"Shit!" Simpson answered smiling. "I'm already in so much trouble nothing short of murder could really make things any worse. come on let's go."

Jed rode in a government Blazer with Bob Simpson out to the Santa Fe airport just south of town. Simpson assured Jed that if he was impressed by the size of the abandoned mines on the ground then his mind would be blown from the air.

Jed and Bob Simpson parked the Blazer beside the small control tower at the Santa Fe airport and walked into the FAA office to file a flight plan. After signing the log book for the state helicopter Bob Simpson motioned for Jed to follow him. The two men walked across the single runway to the state aircraft hanger.

Bob Simpson unlocked the sliding door to a Viet Nam era Huey helicopter parked in front of the hangar and climbed on board. Jed followed and was surprised to see Simpson sit down in the pilot seat and put on a flight helmet with his name stenciled on it.

"Are you the pilot?" Jed asked as he tightened his seat belt.

"I am indeed," Simpson answered with an un-settling maniacal smile. "I flew these puppies through three tours in the Nam and I sort of do the state a favor by doing my own flying for the bureau."

Jed watched as Simpson went through the pre-flight checks and started the engines. As the blades began to build RPMs Jed was amazed to see Simpson pull out a plastic baggie from his flight jacket pocket and begin to roll what appeared to be a joint. Simpson rolled a tight little cigarette, licked both ends and stuck it in the elastic band around his flight helmet. He turned to Jed and gave him the thumbs up signal and Jed returned the gesture.

With that Simpson flashed the maniacal grin again and lifted off. At about 300 feet above the ground Simpson turned the craft westward, angled the nose down and began to accelerate toward the Jemez Mountains. In a matter of seconds the gently rolling plains beneath them gave way to the 800 foot deep gorge of the Rio Grande in White Rock Canyon.

As they crossed the gorge and headed toward the Pajarito Plateau Bob Simpson pulled the illicit cigarette from his helmet and lit it with a Zippo lighter. He inhaled deeply then thrust the smoking cigarette toward Jed.

For a second Jed looked at the joint as though he didn't know what to do with it. Simpson continued to hold it out while he flew the aircraft with his left hand. Jed finally reached out and took it and partook of the sacrament. The image of Mount Taylor grew larger by the minute as they silently passed the joint in the noisy cockpit.

By the time Bob Simpson crushed the resin stained roach Jed could clearly make out the massive scar of the Ratbox Mine. Jed could not believe the scale of the devastation. The view from the air was certainly worthwhile. It looked to Jed as though some great plow had carved a furrow in the earth and sky blue poison water now filled the void.

Jed could see a dust plume from the pit and adjacent waste piles blowing right into Paguate. He could also see great flocks of sheep watering from the tribal reservoir at the east end of the pit.

As the helicopter flew on past the southern most peaks of the sacred mountain Jed recognized the trail he and Lucy had ridden on as they crossed Rinconada Canyon. On the west side of the mountain another facet of the complete picture of mining and milling impacts became apparent.

The huge mill tailings at Python, Grubstake, and Aron McCall as well as the forests of mine headframes in Ambrosia lake were apparent in one long disheartening vista.

As Bob Simpson swung the helicopter to the north Jed saw the blue roofed hogan that had been the home of Lucy's sister. Perhaps because of the joint, or his clear view of the extent of the poisoned land Jed was moved very near to tears by the sight of the hogan so close to the deadly sands of the Aron McCall mill.

Bob Simpson must have seen this because he turned the helicopter back toward the south and flew along the west flank of Mt. Taylor toward I-40. As he crossed the interstate highway he banked hard back to the east and flew in low over the malpais.

As Jed looked out at the blackened landscape through barely restrained tears he suddenly thought of the old legend about this lava flow. He remembered that according to the legend a great evil pueblo had existed on what had been a wide and fertile plain before the mountain erupted and filled it with fiery molten rock. As Jed looked out on this rugged wilderness of jagged basaltic lava 200 feet thick and thought of the old story of justice done by way of the volcano and with the skilled intervention of the Chaco priests a very wild idea began to develop.

It was as though the particular circumstances of his present life had somehow conspired to plant the seed of this wild idea in the fertile ground of Jed's mind. There was no stopping it now. The combination of circumstance and imagination had formed a mental zygote. This wild embryonic idea was growing already and no force on earth could stop it. Jed was crying no longer. He was in fact smiling as he nourished the wild growing thought.

As Jed sat silently smiling he reasoned that if in fact the pueblo culture had long ago mastered the art of manipulating the forces of nature to bring the rains when needed why then would they not also know ways to control natural forces within the earth.

Jed had no doubts after more than 20 years of studying ancient and modern pueblo ways that they indeed did exercise considerable control over natural events through their annual cycle of ceremonies.

He was absolutely convinced that within the great secret body of pueblo knowledge there was a way to cause a volcano to erupt and bleed a new and fresh skin over whatever wretched and evil thing had been wrought on the earth by stupid human beings.

The nature of the only possible solution to this massive act of stupidity around Mt. Taylor became obvious to Jed.

He had to find the cacique or caciques who would perform the proper dance and cause the mountain to erupt and cleanse the land.

Jed knew the knowledge must still be present in the oral tradition and he knew he had to find it. Jed felt strengthened and renewed as the idea grew and took form in his mind. He knew now that no government on earth had the will or the power to even seriously try to eliminate the poison.

He saw quite clearly that it is the nature of western style power structures to facilitate destruction for the profit of a few and to move from one wasted land to another doing the same until nothing is left.

It was not in the nature of our government to heal land or care for the people who live closest to it. It is only the culture which runs contrary to our western European ways, the Native Americans that have the built in capacity to nurture and heal land.

Jed Flyway knew what his vision quest was all about now. He was to take this wild idea hatched in his mind and seek out the only people who could possibly accomplish it. It was crazy and it ran contrary to all accepted norms of thought and precisely because of that he knew it would work if only he had the will and the stamina to stay with the quest.

It was the lights of Santa Fe emerging from the twilight that brought Jed back to present time and space. The helicopter was crossing White Rock Canyon again and dropping into the airport.

Jed was quiet on the ride back to town. In a way he felt higher than he had after smoking the joint three hours earlier.

As the two men pulled into the parking lot on Don Gaspar, Bob Simpson broke the silence.

"Jed I'm sorry I don't have the answers you're looking for. I just wanted you to see the extent of the damage out there. It would take billions of dollars and a great deal of will to accomplish anything and the government is not providing enough of either. I'm real sorry about the pain this mess has caused your loved ones. Many people have suffered the same way and I'm real sorry for all of them too. What else can I say?"

"Hey Listen," Jed answered shrugging his shoulders. "Its sure not your fault all this happened. I believe you'd fix it if you could. I don't expect anymore that any government agency will or even can clean it up. And hey . . . you gave me a view of this that I never would have had otherwise. Thanks a lot for that."

Bob Simpson smiled and held out his arm to shake Jed's hand. "No problem hombre. Glad to do it."

The two men turned and walked away from each other into the growing darkness.

Just as Jed turned the corner onto the Paseo Bob Simpson shouted out to him, "Maybe the mountain will erupt again and take care of all of this." Jed smiled and waived and said quietly, "Yea . . . maybe it will."

Jed spent the next two months working on archaeology contracts mainly on the Pajarito Plateau near Bandelier National Monument. He knew he would need the money to finance his quest for caciques which he never really stopped thinking about.

Jed was also thinking about his reunion with Lucy when she got out of school for the summer. He could scarcely wait to tell her about his vision and his plans to find caciques who could help fulfill the vision.

The sights and smells of New Mexico never seemed so brilliant and strong to Jed as during those two months. The aimless man who had drifted through the last decade with no particular direction or purpose now had a wild vision and a new love driving him.

He was whole for the first time in his life and he knew where he was going and why. He was sober, straight, and in love and it was good.

CHAPTER IV-THE QUEST BEGINS

The late spring snows had given way to early thunderstorms by June. Jed's contract work in the Bandelier country was nearly complete. He had located and mapped the extent of 16 previously unknown pueblo sites and had only to complete the final reports for the Park Service.

Lucy had written to Jed that she would meet him in Santa Fe by the second week in June after spending a few days with her grandparents in Torreon.

When the day finally arrived Jed was at the bus station early. When he saw Lucy in her jeans, flannel shirt, and leather wrapped braids his breath was taken short. He picked her up off the bus station platform with his embrace and kissed her with the urgency of a starving man given his favorite meal.

It took at least fifteen minutes to walk the hundred feet or so to Jed's truck. Every few steps Jed would stop and kiss Lucy again.

Finally Lucy grabbed Jed by the collar and said, "Hey! I'm glad to see you too. . . But I'm hungry. . . for food . . . and before you start undressing me here on the street I think we should eat."

Jed stepped back, chuckled for a moment then sighed, "Are you sure? Couldn't we just lay down here in the back of the truck for a while before we eat?"

"No way belagana," Lucy answered rolling her eyes skyward. "First we eat, then we get behind closed doors where I intend to use your body without mercy."

Jed raised his hands in a gesture of surrender. "All right," he said. "I know when I've been licked . . . all over."

Lucy slapped him gently before climbing into the truck.

Jed and Lucy laughed and joked as he threaded his way through the narrow streets of the barrio to the Chacon Cabron Cafe. Lucy consumed a double order of blue corn enchiladas while Jed ate one relleno and drank four margaritas.

When the two lovers finally got to Jed's place he proceeded to make up for many months of absence from Lucy. A trail of their clothes began at the front door and ended shortly before the bedroom.

Jed kissed Lucy from the bottom of her feet to the top of her head, spending more time at some strategic locations than others, but leaving no part untouched.

It was past three AM before they both slipped into sleep in a limp tangled mass of limbs on top of wet cotton sheets.

It was late morning before the bright sunshine through the skylight and the birdsongs outside their window stirred the tangled lovers.

Jed slithered out of bed first and built a pot of coffee before returning to the bedroom and attempting to renew the activities of the night before.

Jed began by kissing the inside of Lucy's thigh but she pulled away and moaned, "Jed honey, I'm sore. Let me recover a while. Its been a long time since my body has been used in these ways . . . ok?" She sat up and kissed Jed gently.

He looked at her dark brown nipples and moaned.

"Ok babe," he said with a deep breath. "What would you like for breakfast?"

"Something light," she answered quietly. "I'm still full of enchiladas from last night."

Jed smiled and nodded as he walked into the kitchen.

He returned in a few minutes with a steaming cup of coffee and a hot apricot pastry. As they were enjoying their breakfast and smiling at one another Jed's telephone rang.

Jed indicated with a gesture that they should ignore it but after a dozen or so rings Lucy reached over and answered, "Hello, Jed Flyway's place."

A female voice on the other end of the line responded, "Ooohhh, well, is Jed available please? Tell him its his dear friend Christie."

Lucy thrust the phone toward Jed and said in a business like tone, "Its your dear friend Christie, Jed."

Jed took the phone and groaned, "What is it?"

"Well I can tell you're busy Jed," Christie began. "But I wanted to invite you to a party tonight at Jake Flynn's on Canyon Road."

"Thank you Christie, but you are correct. I'm busy and I really don't have time for a party tonight."

"Wait a minute Jed," Christie continued in her usual persistent manner. "This is a very important and elegant event. I really think you ought to be there. And you must bring your friend. Every one will want to see who has stolen all your time and changed your life."

"No, Christie!" Jed responded sternly. "I don't want to go and I'm sure my friend would not enjoy a Canyon Road party."

Lucy touched Jed on the shoulder and shook her head vigorously in an affirmative gesture.

Christie continued, "Well, Jed, if you're ashamed to be seen in public with your mystery love then I guess there's nothing I can do to change your mind."

Jed turned crimson with anger and shouted into the phone, "I'll be there damn it! What time?"

Christie giggled, "Nineish would be fine. See you there love . . . ciao."

Jed slammed down the phone and fumed, "That God damn puta cabrona."

"I can hardly wait to meet her," Lucy said batting her eyelashes.

Jed looked at Lucy still sitting naked in bed and quickly forgot Christie. He kissed her and then he said, "Lucy I want to talk to you about some important things that have happened since our ride around Tsoodzix."

"Ok sweetie," Lucy said smiling. "Tell me all about it. Did you find a nice belagana government man who will make truth, justice, and the American way prevail in Navajo land?"

Jed glared at Lucy and answered, "No! You were right. There is no nice government program out there poised and ready to make things right, and there never will be. But there is a way to cleanse the earth and the answer has always been here and its the Indian people who have it."

Lucy looked at Jed with raised eyebrows and doubt in her eyes.

"Jed we already tried to drive you belaganas out of the country and it didn't work. That's why we were driven onto our concentration camps they call reservations. The Indian view of the world is about 180 degrees contrary to the European view and that is the basis of the problem. We may have heart and soul and be close to the land but you have all the money and the guns."

Jed nodded affirmatively.

"This is all true Lucy. . . but there are some things the Indians have that have never been stolen or destroyed by the Europeans. You have thousands of years of contact with the Great Spirit and the grandfathers. While the Europeans were busy developing the technology of destruction and the politics of deceit, Indian holy people were perfecting a close relationship with the forces of nature. The Indians were able to hold onto the ceremonies and the dances that influence all natural events. It is that very knowledge that is the only hope for saving this world from the ravages of European greed."

Lucy looked at Jed for a few moments then reached out and touched his face. "Jed I have a very strange feeling about what I believe you are thinking. It scares me. It scares me because I think you may be right. But I don't think you understand what you are getting into. The Navajos borrowed most of their religion and beliefs about the spirit world from the Pueblos. But there are some areas of their beliefs that we have always avoided because they are too strange and powerful and dangerous. People have been hurt and even killed by Anasazi chindis. The Anasazi were a very advanced people. They discovered things that no one even today can understand. Their knowledge and their power may have led to their downfall, and trying to find some of that power today could lead to your downfall."

Jed looked quietly into Lucy's eyes before he spoke again.

"Lucy," he finally said. "I appreciate your concern and I understand the risk, but I cannot simply forget what I have seen. A great wrong has been done to the earth and the people who live closest to it. I had a chance to fly over the country we rode in a few weeks ago. It looked hopeless to me from that vantage point. But as I flew over the malpais I remembered the story of the town and the culture and the evil that lies buried beneath that lava flow. For the first time in my life I felt filled with the spirit of purpose. I felt real and whole and I knew in an instant that there was a way to make the earth new and I felt very strongly that this was my quest and my vision to accomplish for all the earth."

Lucy leaned back onto a pillow and asked Jed, "How do you plan to do this?"

Jed thought a minute then answered slowly, "I'm not real sure how to go about this. . . but I thought if you're willing we could go out to your home country and maybe ask someone there for advice about this quest. Maybe we could talk to a holy man or a hatathlis or whatever you call the wise ones, if you know of any, who might be able to give some advice."

Lucy sighed and nodded, "Sure Jed . . . we can go out there and give it a try. I don't see how it could hurt. And I can see there's no talking you out of this."

"No," Jed quickly responded. "I'm not going to give this up. I have a chance to really make a difference for once in my life and I'm not going to let it slip by without trying. I want you to go along with me in this thing Lucy. You're a big part of me and this quest . . . but if you decide at any point to drop out I'll understand."

Lucy smiled and said, "I'm with you hostene. Its crazy and its dangerous but for some reason I feel like you just might succeed."

Jed and Lucy spent most of the day together in bed loving each other and enjoying their closeness. Shortly before sunset they finally dressed and drove up into the mountains above town to a point where they had a clear view of the deepening colors in the west.

The view was magnificent and expansive. They could see every mountain range from the Manzanos in the south to the San Juans in the north. In the middle of the vista just north of where the sun touches the horizon at this time of year was Tsoodzix. Jed could look at nothing else but the sacred mountain and the raven haired woman beside him.

Jed and Lucy left the mountains in time to arrive fashionably late at Jake Flynn's Canyon Road party. Jake Flynn was a Texan who had made a fortune in oil in the early seventies and who now spent his surplus money on art for his gallery on the plaza and on lavish parties.

As Jed pulled up in front of Flynn's walled adobe compound a parking valet in a tux and white gloves approached the dusty pickup looking as though something disagreeable had landed in his nostrils.

"Are you here for Mr. Flynn's party?" he asked in a doubtful tone.

"That's right." Jed answered with a grin.

"Oh," The valet groaned. "May I park your . . .truck . . .sir?"

"No thanks," Jed answered. "I always park on the street pointed in the direction of my best chance of escape. And besides, my truck doesn't like being parked with Volvos."

The valet nodded and walked away with a fixed sneer on his face.

Jed and Lucy parked and walked through the garden gate archway across the meticulously landscaped grounds and into Flynn's refurbished 200 year old hacienda.

The sunken living room was packed with tight little groups of people dressed to the Ts in southwestern sheik. In the center of the huge room was a margarita fountain bubbling forth out of a pueblo wedding vessel held by a nude female sculpture that looked more Greek than Indian.

Along one entire wall of the room a long hand made Mexican table was covered with every imaginable type of hors d'oevre as well as neat rows of blue corn enchiladas and sopapillas.

The finger food on two large round trays was arranged in the shape of Kokopelli, the hump backed flute player of pueblo mythology. Along the opposite wall was a matching table covered with a multitude of liquors and wines.

Through the open French doors leading to the back yard more people were gathered around fountains and sculptures. A string quartet in formal attire provided the background music for this lavish spectacle.

Lucy, who had been looking the whole scene over since she arrived grabbed Jed by the elbow.

"I don't know about you," she whispered. " But I think we should load up on some of that food before these people eat it all up."

"Sure babe," Jed answered. "Go load up, I'll be right with you. I want to get a drink first."

Lucy moved toward the food table and Jed headed for the liquor trying to decide what would best mask the feeling of discomfort he always developed at this sort of affair. As usual there were too many choices and Jed finally decided that his best bet was to take the largest beer glass he could find and fill it to the rim from the margarita fountain.

As he was filling his glass he felt a set of arms wrap around his waist and the unmistakable sensation of female breasts pressed hard against his back. He turned around expecting to see Lucy but instead saw a tiny red head in a flimsy cotton halter top.

"Christie," Jed said with a tone of combined embarrassment and disgust.

"Yes dear," she answered still clinging to him. "I'm so glad you decided to come. I can't wait to show you off to some of my friends here. Everyone is so in to Indian things and you know more than anyone about that stuff. And you're sooooo cute too."

Before Jed could respond Lucy walked up holding a silver plate full of enchiladas and shrimp. She looked at Jed and the woman clinging to him and said, "Jed, I don't know if you noticed it but you have a strange growth on your back."

Christie let go of Jed and looked at Lucy. "Oh my Jed," she said smiling. "This must be the girl you've been telling me about. Well she's every bit as charming as you said. Very good to meet you, dear, my name is Christie. I've known Jed here since you were a very small child, I should think."

Lucy looked down at Christie's outstretched hand and continued to eat her enchiladas. In a moment Christie withdrew her hand and said, "Well. . . very good to meet you dear. I didn't mean to offend you. You know," she continued with a little laugh, "Jed's really not worth this much concern. There are a hundred others just like him out there for the taking. You'll see that when you've had a little more experience."

Lucy chewed her enchilada thoughtfully for a moment then said, "You know what I think lady. I think if you really felt that way you wouldn't be acting like such a bitch." Lucy smiled and walked away toward the patio.

Jed turned up his drink and quickly filled it again and followed after her. "I'm sorry about that." he began when he caught up with her.

Lucy held her fingers up to Jed's lips and said, "Forget it babe. She's the one with the problem, not you."

Lucy and Jed wandered around for a while saying hello to some of Jed's more courteous friends and trying to enjoy the art and music.

At one point a tall man in alligator boots and an immaculately clean cowboy hat walked up to them.

"Are you Jed Flyway, son?" he asked in a strong Texas drawl while shaking Jed's hand.

"Yea . . . that's right," Jed answered.

"Well son I am damn glad to meet you. Jake Flynn's my name. This here is my place."

"Well . . . its very nice," Jed said politely while Lucy nodded agreement. Like many Texans, Jake Flynn could not be quiet for long and his favorite course of conversation was the big deal.

"Hell, son, this is very fortuitous meetin' you here. I been wantin' to contact you about looking at some pots I bought up in Utah. They're supposed to be a thousand years old and I'd be willing to pay you any price to verify that and tell what you can about where they were made, who made 'em and shit like that. I've got some buyers in Europe that'll give anything for bona fide old Indian stuff like that."

"Well. . . uh," Jed began trying to find an answer that would not be too offensive. "Maybe we can talk some more later. . . uh. . . . I'm pretty busy right now."

"Why hell yes, son! Ya'll enjoy yourselves right now. We'll talk business later." He slapped Jed on the back and walked off into the crowd laughing. Jed finished off his second big margarita and said, "Its mother fuckers like that who cause whole pueblo sites to be bulldozed. Just getting busted for dealing in stolen pots is really not enough for him. He should be strung up on poles and shot through the gut with sacred arrows."

Lucy looked at Jed for a moment then ran her fingers through his hair and said, "I think its time to go Jed." Jed nodded agreement and they both made their way through the crowd and back out to the street where Jed's truck was parked.

That evening they reminded each other once again what was most important. Their love drove all memory of the trite Santa Fe artista elite from their minds.

Jed was up early the next morning loading his truck with camping gear and food. After a hearty New Mexico breakfast they were off to Navajo country. Jed, as usual, took the back roads over the Jemez and Nacimiento Mountains and emerged on the edge of Navajo Land at the norteno town of Cuba. It was only a short drive through the sagebrush and badlands to the Torreon Chapter country where Lucy had been raised.

Lucy knew all the elders and holy men in this area. She directed Jed through a maze of dirt tracks to an isolated stone hogan in the middle of a sea of rolling sagebrush covered hills.

"This is Fred Tohachini's place," she announced to Jed. "He's the oldest man in the Torreon Chapter and knows more about Anasazi than any Navajo I know."

Jed understood that Navajo protocol dictated that they both remain in the truck until the occupant of the hogan saw fit to emerge and either greet them or run them off.

As they waited Lucy warned Jed, "You know most Navajos don't want anything to do with Anasazi. They avoid the ruins and they won't even pick up a pot sherd. There's a real good chance that Fred won't even want to talk to us about Anasazi magic and ceremonies."

"I understand the risk," Jed assured her. "But I think its worth a try starting out here in country and with people you're familiar with."

After about a forty minute wait the weather beaten blue door of the hogan opened and an ancient looking old man hobbled out leaning heavily on a crooked cottonwood cane. He looked warily at the truck for a moment until Lucy rolled down her window and greeted him in Navajo. He returned the greeting and asked Lucy what she wanted.

She explained that her companion was on a spiritual quest and wanted some advice. The old man looked hard at Jed.

Jed thought that he looked as old as the land he lived on. His shoulder length white hair fluttered in the light wind and his eyes looked like dark tunnels full of mystery. The old man wore a faded turquoise bandana as a headband and around his neck on a leather string hung a small pouch.

The old man finally grunted and pointed toward the open door with his lips. Lucy and Jed followed him inside and all three sat on well worn Navajo rugs that covered the dirt floor.

Lucy handed the old man a sack of oranges and a tin of tobacco as a gift of greeting. After a moment of respectful silence Lucy began to speak to the holy man in Navajo. He nodded and grunted as she spoke and when she was finished he looked at the hogan ceiling and fondled the small leather pouch around his neck.

After a short period of silence he responded to Lucy in Navajo. Lucy in turn nodded and grunted as he spoke. As the old man spoke he gestured in the air with his hands. He carved elegant circles and diagonals and often emphasized a word with an outstretched hand pointing to the west. When he was through speaking he slapped his hands on his thighs and smiled a toothless smile at Lucy.

Lucy stood up and motioned for Jed to follow her. She thanked Fred Tohachini before closing the door.

As they rode back down the dusty two track road Lucy began to explain what Fred had told her.

"I'm kinda surprised," she began. "He wasn't at all shocked at what you want to do. It was as though he'd been expecting someone to do this for a long time. He said that if he were a younger man he would go with you to find the old caciques. And by the way he says they are still out there. Its just a matter of finding them. Fred says we will never find them on this physical plane, and he suggested that it might take some pretty strong medicine to get you to the right place. He told me there's going to be a NAC meeting over in the Chuskas this Saturday night. A guy named Jack Silvercloud will be the roadman for that meeting. He's a Commanche I think, from Oklahoma. I don't know him but I do have some relatives over in Tohatchee and Two Grey Hills who will probably go to that meeting. If you want to give it a try and go to that peyote meeting I'll try to get you in. Fred seemed to think that would be a good place to start."

Jed thought about the proposition for a few minutes as they bounced along the dirt track then announced, "Why not? I haven't had any PIE-O-TIE in a long spell. It might be just the ticket. We can puke and piss all over ourselves and drift off together to the land where the old caciques dwell."

Lucy turned quickly to Jed and said, "Wait a minute hostene. I'll go with you on this crazy quest because I think it might just work. But you can have the medicine. I'll watch and enjoy the good food they always have at NAC meetings. You can drift off to whatever land you want to . . . just as long as you come back . . . in one piece."

Jed smiled at Lucy and agreed that she was probably right as usual.

Jed turned back onto the pavement just before Pueblo Pintado and headed west for the Chaco Mesa. All the way across the mesa Jed pointed out the canyons with cliff houses and good petroglyphs. He had been among the first archeologists to conduct systematic surveys of the Chaco Mesa country and he knew something about every canyon on the mesa.

He was so busy telling Lucy about the signal buttes he had found all over the Chaco country that he didn't notice the tribal police car parked behind a boulder in the mouth of a small canyon. It was several more minutes before Jed noticed the flashing red lights in his rear view mirror and realized it was he the policeman was after.

Jed pulled over to the wide shoulder of the highway just before the road dropped off the western escarpment of the Chaco Mesa. He fumbled for his license as he watched the burley Navajo policeman in his side mirror, walking slowly toward his truck.

The tribal officer was dressed like an overweight Nazi storm trooper and wore steel rimmed mirrored sun glasses. Jed smiled and offered his license to the officer when he arrived at the truck window. He didn't take the license and he said nothing.

Jed finally asked, "Was I speeding? I didn't think this old truck still had it in her."

Still the officer said nothing. He began to walk around the truck slowly. When he got to the passenger side window he stopped for a moment and seemed to be looking at Lucy then at Jed. He continued his circuit of the truck walking very slowly until he was once again standing beside Jed.

Both Lucy and Jed were by this time beginning to get very nervous about this silent sentinel of justice. Jed stole a quick glance at Lucy. She shrugged her shoulders.

Finally the officer moved in very close to Jed's face and spoke. "Where's your dope?"

Jed looked at the cop with amazement and answered honestly, "I don't have any dope. You can look anywhere you like. I have nothing to hide."

The cop began to breathe in harder as he barked at Jed, "Are you trying to tell me you don't have any reefer in this truck?"

"Absolutely none!" Jed answered becoming seriously concerned now.

"Then both of you get out of this truck!" he bellowed. "Now go over there and stand by my car!"

Jed and Lucy complied without question.

The officer followed them and once again with his face in Jed's he asked, "You are absolutely sure you have no dope in that truck?"

"None," Jed answered with sweat pouring down his face. "Nothing at all."

The officer looked at Jed again and muttered, "No dope, huh?" He then reached up and pulled off his mirrored glasses and said in a light and cheerful tone, "Then we'll just have to smoke some of mine."

Jed and Lucy looked at each other in disbelief as the officer reached inside his patrol car and pulled out a beaded medicine pouch from under the seat. He loaded a hand carved juniper pipe with what appeared to be sensimilla buds. He held the pipe high in salute to father sky then he acknowledged mother earth and the four cardinal directions before lighting the bowl.

The sweet smell of powerful marijuana drifted in the light breeze. The officer inhaled deeply and then handed the pipe to Jed. He accepted then took a polite hit and handed the pipe to Lucy. At first she held up her hand and indicated she wanted nothing to do with it. But Jed let her know with facial expressions that he thought she should join the circle to placate the keeper of Navajo justice.

She complied reluctantly and passed the pipe back to its owner. This process continued for three or four rounds and by the time the pipe was put away in its rightful spot in the medicine pouch, Jed and Lucy were swaying in the breeze just like the sparse grasses beside the road.

The officer slumped against his patrol car and looked off quietly across the vast plain to the west. For a long while he did not speak. The grasses crackled as they bent in the breeze. Somewhere in the vague distance insects buzzed. Lizards scurried from rocks to bushes as hawks soared above in a dazzling blue sky.

Finally the keeper of Navajo law and order turned toward Jed and Lucy who had both forgotten the circumstances under which they had arrived in this situation. He began to speak as though he was continuing an ongoing conversation.

"You know," he said raising an arm skyward as he spoke. "I spend many hours out here on this highway, driving, watching, patrolling. . . and I never get a chance to talk to people. Sometimes I don't even see people for days. Then when I do, its to give someone a ticket or arrest a drunk. Everyone believes I'm the heavy . . . a bad guy. . . a real agency asshole. I'm a real person and I'm lonely."

The officer raised both hands to the sun and continued.

"I have ideas and I have heart. I have visions that are real and important. I walk the warriors path just as the old ones. I am strong and I walk the path with heart. I am a man. Will you hear me? Will you listen to my visions?"

Tears rolled down his cheeks as he asked these questions. Jed looked at Lucy as though he had no idea what to say. Lucy took a deep breath and spoke, "Yes hostene, we will listen. Tell us of your visions. They are real and important."

The Navajo peace officer wiped his eyes and sat down in the sand. "Thank you sister," he said with genuine appreciation. "Thank you."

He drew a deep breath and looked off to the west across the wide and empty plain between the Chaco Mesa and Hosta Butte.

"One day as I sat here in this spot, smoking alone, I looked out over that llano and saw the gathering camps of all the human beings. All of them. I watched as all the holy men from all the camps of the human beings came together for a council. As I watched them I saw that all their differences began to fade and they all became bright points of light like stars. Soon the lights all came together into one great bright light on the llano. This great white light grew until it began to cover everything. It became the whole llano, then the mesas and all the human beings. . . even me. I felt strong and lite and soon

I was moving through the sky with the great light and it was becoming everything and I was a part of everything. And then I got a call on my radio. Someone in Crownpoint had pissed on another persons sheep dog and I had to go break up a fight and I lost that vision, and I never got it back."

The officer stretched his arms and yawned as he looked at his watch. "Oh!" he said with a grunt. "My shift is over I gotta go. Mighty nice to meet you folks."

And with that he waived and sped off in his patrol car.

Lucy and Jed stood silently on the roadside for several minutes. Neither could believe what had just happened and both of them were so stoned they weren't really sure what had happened. Finally Lucy rubbed her eyes pushed back her hair and said, "Jed, I'm thirsty . . . lets go."

Jed nodded and walked behind Lucy to the truck. Lucy hung her head out of the open window as Jed slowly drove on down the road. Jed stopped at the White Horse Trading Post and bought two Pepsis and a sack of apples, then he proceeded on toward Crownpoint.

Lucy was finding great solace in watching the clouds with her head against the door handle as Jed turned off the pavement onto the Chaco Canyon Road. The bumpy dirt road made it difficult to maintain her position so she sat up and began to talk.

"What are we gonna do until Saturday?"

Jed smiled and shoved back his bushy hair with his fingers. "Well we can do whatever you like . . . but if you're interested I could show you some nice cliff dwellings outside the park. We could camp there and explore some canyons. . . and whatever else might come to mind." Lucy grinned and nodded and that was good enough for Jed.

They spent the next few days enjoying each other and exploring unexcavated pueblo ruins and cliff dwellings. They found a beautiful spring in a grove of cottonwoods hidden in a box canyon. They bathed each other with diligence and lay in the sun together on the damp sand where the spring disappeared into the ground. They watched hawks soaring and they watched each other and they fell deeper into love with each passing hour.

Early Saturday morning while the cool and clear light still dominated the world Jed and Lucy left the Chaco country and headed west along reservation tracks toward the Chuska Mountains. This beautiful highland oasis rises abruptly from the parched and overgrazed plains of the eastern Navajo Reservation.

As Jed watched the forested massif of the Chuskas growing larger with each westward mile he felt both excitement and trepidation. He knew there was a chance that he would not be allowed to participate in the peyote meeting, and he knew that if he was, there was no predicting what might occur.

He had chewed on his fair share of bitter cactus in the late sixties when he and his Taos pals would sit in on kiva peyote meetings or hold their own in Arroyo Hondo. He had felt the good, the bad, and the ugly that could come of using psycotropic tools for self improvement. He had decided some ten years earlier that these tools were too powerful for him and he hadn't even considered them again until now.

It was nearly noon by the time they reached Toadlena at the base of the Chuskas. Jed waited in the truck while Lucy went into the Toadlena Chapter House to inquire about the whereabouts of her uncle, Eddie Yazzie. She was told he could probably be found at a crafts stand near the post office. They drove over to a cluster of makeshift open fronted sheds and found Lucy's uncle selling silver bracelets and conchos.

Jed talked to a white haired weaver at the next stall as Lucy spoke to her uncle about the peyote meeting. Lucy motioned for Jed to come over and he was introduced to her uncle who offered a feeble Navajo handshake and a pleasant "ya tah".

Lucy explained that Jack Silvercloud was setting up for the night's meeting in a canyon above Mexican Springs and that her uncle recommended they get on over there to be sure of a space in the meeting.

"This is a real important meeting for the folks over there," Lucy explained. "They need the grandfathers and Jesus to help with a witch problem they're having up there."

"Witch problem?" Jed asked.

"Yea, it seems that a lot of livestock and dogs have been killed and strangely dismembered around there and some witches up in the mountains are believed responsible. Everyone has their witch flags flying around the hogans, but it hasn't been enough, so they're gonna speak to the grandfathers about it tonight."

"Hmmmm. . ." Jed began while scratching his chin. "Do you think I'll be welcome at this meeting?"

"Oh you'll be welcome," Lucy answered. "Its just a matter of reserving a space. We better vamanouse on over there."

Lucy kissed her uncle on the head and he handed Jed a small silver medallion with a flying thunderbird above a crescent moon strung on purple yarn. Jed put on the medallion and thanked Eddie Yazzie who nodded and smiled at him with a strange twinkle in his eye that made Jed feel like this old man knew what was to come this evening.

The Native American Church was enjoying a great revival in Navajo country. Many religions were vying for the souls of this most populous of all Indian tribes but the peyote church was by far the most popular with both old traditionals and young militants.

The NAC practice and ceremonies were still substantially the same as established by Quana Parker, the halfblood Commanche that terrorized Texas and New Mexico for two decades before suddenly agreeing to settle down on an Oklahoma reservation. Quana became very successful and influential in the white world, but by formalizing the use of peyote as a sacrament in Indian religious practice he gave all Native Americans a lasting link with their traditional past.

Lucy and Jed bounced on up the dusty road to Mexican Springs and found the NAC meeting camp in the mouth of Yei Canyon. Several Navajo men were gathering firewood and making last minute preparations in and around the sacred white tepee. A very different looking Indian man wearing a red silk cowboy shirt and sunglasses was leaning against a white convertible 1964 Cadillac.

Jed figured this had to be the Commanche roadman Jack Silvercloud. As Lucy and Jed approached him the roadman looked up and smiled, revealing a mouth full of gold rimmed teeth and a small silver star on one incisor.

"Yah ta hey," he said in a friendly tone with a strange combination of Indian and southern accents.

"Yah ta hey," Jed answered while shaking his hand gently.

"So. . ." Jack Silvercloud began still grinning broadly. "You want to sit in the meeting tonight . . . no?"

"Yes," Jed answered. "I would like that very much. I need the help of the grandfathers for a mission I'm on."

"Uh huh," Silvercloud said nodding his head. "I see that you are on a vision quest and you do need the help of the grandfathers . . . and Jesus . . . and all your relations. . . amen. Ho. . . yes brother you are welcome to take the medicine with us tonight . . . ho. And may you find the help you need."

"Can we do anything to help before the meeting starts?" Lucy asked.

"Yes sister," Silvercloud answered. "You can help with the gathering of wood and water and juniper incense."

The balance of the afternoon was spent helping the other participants in these and other preparations for the meeting.

By the time sunset gave way to twilight many other participants and their families had arrived. A large fire was lit near the tables which were arranged under a brush arbor and were now covered with the makings of a feast. People stood around the fire and laughed and gossiped as they waited for the meeting to begin.

As a brilliant half moon rose over the canyon rim roadman Silvercloud appeared from behind a cluster of junipers dressed in beaded white buckskins. Behind him walked his Navajo assistant carrying a bulging white canvas sack. Everyone watched silently as he circled the outside of the sacred tepee four times then opened the door flap.

Silvercloud stepped inside the tepee and turned to the left and walked slowly halfway around the interior and sat down behind a crescent shaped earthen alter that faced the entry. As Jed watched through the open door flap he saw the roadman remove an enormous perfectly symmetrical peyote button from a beaded pouch hanging on his sash. He placed this grandfather peyote in the center of the crescent shaped alter and then placed an eagle bone whistle to his lips and blew four shrill blasts on it.

At that signal all those who wanted to participate in the meeting began to approach the tepee. Jed said goodbye to Lucy and joined the other 15 participants. As each person entered the tepee they turned to the left and walked around the perimeter of the sacred space and took seats on either side of the roadman. When everyone was seated the assistant began to light cigarettes with a fire stick and pass them around to all participants. Jed and all the others puffed on their cigarettes which were primarily tobacco as far as Jed could tell.

When all had breathed the one breath of the grandfather the roadman smiled and began to speak. "Grandfather," he said in a strong voice that seemed to echo in the tepee. "We are here tonight to seek your blessings in a sacred way. We all have needs that we know you can fulfill. We are all pitiful creatures here on earth who need your help. We ask you in the name of all that is holy and sacred to hear our prayers grandfather and give us what we need."

Then to Jed's amazement the roadman recited a slightly modified version of the Lord's Prayer which ended with the phrase "and to all my relations. . . amen!"

With that the canvas sack of peyote began its clockwise journey around the tepee along with a smudge bowl containing a smoldering mixture of sage and sweet grass. Each person whether they elected to eat a button or not held the sack as they spoke the first of what would be many prayers specifying what was desired by them of the grandfathers.

Jed managed to consume three of the bitter dried cacti on the first round as he prayed to grandfather for guidance in his quest for the knowledge of the ancient ones. After the first round the honored water bearing woman entered the tepee and offered spring water to all. Before the second round of the sacred medicine, the roadman sang a song in a strange native tongue that seemed somehow familiar to Jed. As he sang he accompanied himself on a small water filled kettle drum. The little drum was passed along with the peyote on the second round.

As the medicine began its second clockwise journey around the tepee Jed began to feel the first subtle hints of change in his perceptions. A slight tingling of the epidermis. Warmth in the area of his heart and some minor gastro intestinal distress. Each participant prayed again as the medicine sack made the circuit. This time it seemed to Jed that the prayers were given with more reverence and new meaning to mother earth, father sky, and to all their relations. . . amen.

As Jed took the medicine the second time his eyes were drawn to the grandfather peyote on the crescent alter. Jed felt himself answer a question that he had not even heard asked. "Yes grandfather," he answered, "I will have three more of your children." Jed pulled three more buttons from the sack and consumed them as he prayed.

"Grandfather!" Jed cried earnestly as his ears began to ring and his vision blurred. "Help me to find the way that surely exists . . . to stop the evil that has been unleashed on this land between the four sacred mountains. Help me grandfather. . . to find the ones who know the path. Help me to find the holy ones who bring the rains and spare the floods and maintain the balance that keeps life on this earth."

Jed sobbed deeply at this point and realized that the two men on either side of him were holding him in a brotherly embrace as he cried. He felt a warmth and a kinship with them that he had never known before in his life. He was strengthened by these feelings and continued his prayer.

"Grandfather, some of the human beings have tried to find the power of creation in the rocks beneath the sacred mountain of the south. They have poisoned the land and the people who live on it with these rocks. I am asking you grandfather to help me find the path . . . the dance that will let the sacred mountain create a new and healthy skin for the land. I know that this has been done in the past and can be done today with the right heart and mind. I am asking you grandfather to help me. I am a pitiful human and I need your power to make this thing happen. Thank you grandfather for this chance. . . .and to all my relations. . . amen."

Jed opened his eyes to a very different scene. The intensity of light was lower yet somehow more vivid. His feeling of kinship for every one and everything in the tepee was overpowering. Most remarkable of all was the fact that he no longer heard human voices at all. As the prayers continued he heard instead the sounds of nature. Running water, wind, frogs and crickets and coyotes. And none of this seemed at all strange to him. He understood exactly what was being expressed by these sounds and it was pure poetry. When the peyote made its third round Jed consumed three more buttons with no difficulty whatsoever.

Jed's perception of available light had been diminishing for some time. Shortly after his ingestion of the third round of peyote his ability to perceive light was reduced to a strange and growing luminescence emanating from father peyote, the large specimen of the cactus in the center of the crescent shaped alter. By that point this did not seem at all strange to Jed. The glowing sky blue light gently illuminated the depressed ridges of the huge peyote button and seemed to pulsate with each breath that Jed took.

As he watched the light with fascination it began to grow and take on the shape of a human. This glowing blue creature of light began to move gently toward Jed. As the light being stood beside him Jed felt a warm and exciting touch on his forehead. Jed's immediate response was to lie on the ground and close his eyes. Jed, or a very important part of Jed, then accepted the light being's unspoken invitation to step outside his body.

Jed did not receive the midnight water, as his physical form lay apparently unconscious on the ground. Lucy who had remained outside was more than a little concerned at seeing the silhouette of Jed through the lighted tepee slump backward and remain prone.

As the water bearing woman left the tepee she walked directly to Lucy and told her that Roadman Silvercloud had asked her to assure Lucy that Jed was fine and in good hands, and that his prayers were being answered.

Jed meanwhile, in another form entirely, was floating effortlessly through space with the light being. As he looked down at the irridescent and glowing landscape he felt himself landing on a huge spire of rock separated by a distance of perhaps 50 yards from a high and rugged mesa.

Along the mesa escarpment, glowing like subdued pink neon Jed saw a large pueblo ruin. This was not any pueblo Jed had ever seen though and he had visited just about all of them. As Jed enjoyed the unearthly beauty before him he suddenly noticed a pack of glowing purple coyotes running across the mesa toward the pueblo. These colorful canines ran around and over every part of the pueblo sniffing and scent marking everything. Finally the pack of coyotes dove through the entry of a kiva and disappeared, except for one. This lone coyote pulsating green and yellow around the mouth and eyes ran to the edge of the cliff opposite Jed.

Jed and the coyote watched each other for a moment and then with a great smear of color the luminescent beast leapt across the gap from the mesa to the rock spire. As Jed looked at the animal in front of him it rolled itself into a ball and sped off with a sound like rolling thunder into a pile of boulders. Jed's curiosity moved him toward the boulders. To his amazement he found an old Indian man sitting in the rock pile smiling. Suddenly it occurred to Jed that he had found a cacique that could help him in his quest. The old man motioned for Jed to sit beside him. Jed looked carefully at the man beside him. He seemed in many ways not unlike any old man from a pueblo even today. His white hair was pulled into the familiar pueblo back knot. He wore a cotton breach cloth held in place by a beautifully woven sash. Around his neck was a necklace made of several braided strands of dark beans with a turquoise thunderbird in front.

There were some rather unusual things about this man though. When Jed looked for more than just a moment into his dark eyes he began to see rapidly moving scenes of clouds and landscape. When he looked away from the mans eyes the scene returned to normal, if in fact anything could be called normal in his present condition. There was also a bright thin band of silver luminescence surrounding the old man.

After a short period of quiet the old cacique began to speak to Jed, or rather to communicate in some fashion as his lips never moved. Nonetheless Jed received this message very clearly.

"Follow me, young warrior."

And so he did follow the cacique as he walked slowly to the center of the spire and stomped four times on the ground. In response to that signal, the rock split open and revealed a kiva ladder leading into a space within the spire illuminated by a pulsating orange glow. The cacique made three false starts before descending the ladder on the fourth. Without hesitation Jed followed the example and entered the sacred space.

Jed followed the cacique on four circuits of the inside of the small circular chamber before sitting beside him in front of the sipapu, the small round hole in the floor of the kiva that is the window between the worlds. As Jed stared into the sipapu it began to glow with an intense white light. Suddenly a beam of white light burst forth from the sipapu. Out of this fountain of light Kachinas began to emerge.

Masked dancers from another world in all their glowing finery. The Kachinas danced and moved around the kiva to a rhythm of mysterious origin. One of the Kachinas wearing a black and white mask with lightning marks stepped to the middle of the kiva and pointed a spruce bough at Jed.

Although there were no words spoken Jed received a very clear message from the lightning Kachina. There is a way, Jed was made to understand, to dance the proper dance and thereby align the forces of nature that control volcanoes just as surely as clouds and rain are controlled by the proper dance.

The dance has been lost by the consumptive cultures and because of this they are at the mercy of a runaway nature spirit. This has led to much death, disease, and despair even while material wealth was being generated.

The lightning Kachina caused Jed to know that there was a way for even he, a member of the consumptive, destructive culture to find the dance of life again. He was made to know also that the way would not just be given to him. He would have to find it and earn it on his own.

He would have to walk the warriors path, thinking and doing good to all things. The task before him was made clear by the Kachina's communication. He had much ground to cover both within himself and on the sacred earth.

As Jed came to the realization of what his task was the Kachinas formed a line and moved in unison toward the sipapu. As each Kachina came near to the fountain of light issuing from the sipapu he assumed a crouched position, leapt into the air and dove headlong into the window to the other worlds. When the last Kachina disappeared through the sipapu the column of light condensed back into the glowing circle Jed had seen when he entered the kiva.

Jed watched as the old cacique stood slowly and climbed up the kiva ladder. He followed him and stood with him on the spire as the hole in the rock closed and the kiva ladder vanished. As the two stood on the spire looking at one another Jed saw a bright circular spot begin to appear on the cacique's forehead. Jed realized the spot of light looked very much like the glowing sipapu in the kiva. He felt a form of communication was coming through this light and being received by what seemed like a similar spot on his own forehead.

In an instant Jed realized that his next task in the quest would be to find the old cacique at his pueblo in the world that he usually moved in. He was also made to understand that any path he took from the spire would lead him safely back to his normal world where his physical body was waiting.

Jed determined that he would simply walk off into space from the rock spire. As he took a fearless step into the charged air of this mystical place a flat rock appeared under his foot. With each step another multicolored, glowing stepping stone appeared. As Jed walked off toward the shimmering horizon the cool tones of night began to give way to a crimson dawn.

In what seemed only a few moments Jed was looking down from his airy perch on the site of the peyote meeting. He was attracted to a thin wisp of smoke that rose from the white tepee. He walked into the column of smoke and felt himself becoming the smoke. At that very moment Lucy awoke from her fitful sleep in the back of Jed's truck and saw a raven flying above the tepee through the smoke.

Inside the tepee Jed's physical form sat upright and accepted a sacred pipe from the roadman. The final prayers were said and the final water was passed within the tepee. The participants stood and filed out of the tepee in a clockwise circle and greeted the new day.

A feast awaited all who were interested in such physical plane activities. Jed could not as yet bring himself to eat. He drank hot black coffee as Lucy more than made up for his lack of appetite. She sampled every dish on the table and those she enjoyed most she returned to at least once. There was steaming fresh frybread, mutton stew, hot stuffed rellenos, rolled enchiladas, tamales, and half a dozen more delectables in more than ample quantity.

When Lucy's appetite for food was finally sated she turned to Jed who was leaning against his truck staring at passing clouds and said, "Let's go down to Gallup and get a room. I didn't sleep too well last night. I was worried about you. I could use some good rest and I'm sure you could too."

Jed continued to stare at the clouds moving across the turquoise firmament. After a few minutes with no response to her suggestion Lucy tried again, "Hello Jed, come in, this is planet earth calling."

Jed turned slowly to look at her and asked, "What is it babe?"

"What it is," she answered placing an arm on his shoulder, "is this: we're both tired and you're spaced and I think we ought to drive down to Gallup and get a motel room so we can rest up . . . and so forth. . . ok?"

"Gallup?" Jed asked wrinkling his brow.

"Right," Lucy answered finishing off a piece of fry bread. "Gallup. The garden spot of the southwest. Indian capitol of the world. Hey its close . . . and it has motels and showers and food. And on the way you can tell me all about what happened last night."

With some reluctance Jed agreed to the plan and he and Lucy were soon rolling back down the dirt road from Yei Canyon toward the dirty black top of the road to Gallup with the unfortunate numerical designation of Highway 666.

The drive down from the Chuskas to Gallup covered territory familiar to both Jed and Lucy. Somehow, though, on this morning everything looked fresh and new to both of them.

Every shimmering heat wave off the multi colored badlands looked like the birth of rainbows swimming into the eternal sea of the brilliant morning sky.

They both knew that the world was truly new for them and that the future would hold revelations unimagined. As Jed retold the events of the previous night they both felt a collective shiver and they knew for certain that the quest had begun.

❖

CHAPTER V-TO CATCH A CACIQUE

As Jed's aged vehicle crossed the triple six bypass over the Rio Puerco and entered Gallup he knew for certian he was back in the physical world. The dirty strip of train tracks between the Rio Puerco and old Route 66 was full of tight little groups of drunken Navajos, some sleeping precariously close to the tracks, others passing brown sack covered bottles of Tokay. Gallup was never pretty but on this day somehow it seemed particularly loathsome.

Jed turned west onto old Route 66 and began to cruise the motel strip. Most of the old motels built in the 40s and 50s had fallen on hard times. They functioned now mainly as short term crash pads and dingy islands of escape from the even dingier town around them.

Route 66 had become a forest of gaudy flashing signs advertising cheap room rates and free HBO. Every building that was not a motel, gas station, or cheap restaurant seemed to be a liquor store or bar. Around every liquor establishment was a resident group of Navajos exhibiting varying degrees of inebriation.

Jed looked at the pitiful, hopeless and sick faces of these Indians and found it hard to believe that these were the same people who he had felt such kinship to in the peyote meeting. He knew though that this sort of scene was common on reservations throughout the country and that groups like the Native American Church were trying hard to restore the lost sense of pride to Indian communities.

For no particular reason Jed pulled into the parking lot of the Palomino Motel.

"Well," he said smiling at Lucy. "Let's see if we can get one of the executive suites."

Jed walked in to the motel office and was immediately hit with the strong smell of curry. He knew as he rang the bell that as is usually the case an East Indian proprietor would soon appear. As expected he soon heard excited dialogue in Hindi behind the curtain that separated the office from the owner's living quarters.

In a moment a small dark man appeared and asked, "You want room for day or night?"

"Well," Jed answered slowly. "Both actually."

"How many are you?" the Hindi man asked in his rapid fire English.

"Uh... its me and my girlfriend." Jed smiled pointing through the window at Lucy.

"Two then?" The proprietor said looking over his check in book as though he had reservations to consider. "I have only room with two beds. That is $23.95 plus tax."

Jed looked at the small man, then looked out the office window at the motel sign where the plastic letters said, "Single $13.95, Double $15.95, Free HBO."

"What about your advertised rate?" Jed asked pointing to the sign.

"Sorry," The man answered. "I have no of these rooms available. Only two beds, $23.95 you want or no?"

Jed looked out at the empty parking lot then at Lucy who was falling asleep in the truck and with a sigh he answered, "All right let's do it."

The Hindi man took Jed's money and handed him a worn brass key with the number 12 scratched into it. Jed moved his truck into the designated parking spot and with only a little difficulty he opened the room door and soon he and Lucy were inside their dingy island refuge making the best of the available amenities.

The shower was small but it worked, and the closeness of a water conservation shower was welcomed by both participants. Afterwards they dried one another and fell naked into one of the creaking old beds and enjoyed some much needed closeness and rest.

Jed fell into a deep and dream filled sleep that lasted without interruption until the following morning. Lucy's sleep was not so sound. Every time a Santa Fe Pacific train streaked by on the tracks across Route 66 she was jolted from her sleep. She was also disturbed by shouting outside their room during the night and a gunshot in the early morning hours. When Jed finally did wake, Lucy was sitting up in the bed, naked, watching a Chuck Norris karate movie with no sound.

"What day is this?" Jed asked rubbing his eyes. "Where are we? What are you watching?"

Lucy turned to Jed and leaning back on one arm she answered, "Welcome to the real world hostene. This is Monday morning in beautiful downtown Gallup. And this guy is the only man in the world that can take out 12 people with one kick. Nice tush too."

Jed dragged himself out of bed and staggered into the bathroom muttering incomprehensibly. He emerged in a few minutes after a shower looking fresh and ready to tackle the world.

As Jed stood in front of the bathroom door drying his hair with a small motel towel Lucy leaned forward to change the TV channel and asked, "What's next Jed?"

He stared at her hindquarters and her full round breasts hanging down as she leaned forward and he knew at once what the immediate answer to that question was. He crawled onto the bed behind her and reached between her legs and up to her breasts. She moaned and sat back against his arm and tightened her thighs. For the next hour and a half there was only one quest to think of and that was the quest for as much of each other as they could get. And in that quest they were quite successful.

Jed and Lucy held each other quietly on the tangled sheets for almost an hour after their breathing returned to normal before a word was said. Finally Lucy repeated an earlier question. "What are we going to do next Jed? Where will we look for your old cacique?"

Jed rubbed Lucy's lumbar curve and looked thoughtful for a few seconds before answering. "I think," he began with a deep breath, "we should go back to the Chuskas and start searching the canyons on the west side . . . between Mexican Springs and Crystal. There's a lot of country there that's never been carefully searched for ruins. For some reason . . . I guess because the peyote meeting was near there I feel like I might find the coyote pueblo there . . . and the cacique."

"Hmmmm," Lucy said turning to look at Jed. "Pueblo del Coyote y cacique viejo. . . no? Is that what we're calling this place and its old sorcerer?"

"Sure," Jed answered. "That's as good a name as any."

"Ok," Lucy said as she stood up and began to search for her clothes. "Let's get with it then Hostene. But first lets get something to eat. I'm starving."

Jed agreed to the hot breakfast idea and he and Lucy ate hearty at Gordo's Mexican Kitchen before they headed north again out of the depressing little town. An hour later found them packing food and sleeping bags in the meadow below Yei Canyon, where the peyote meeting had been. The rapid transition from the harsh reality of Gallup to the stunning beauty of the Chuskas renewed Jed's determination to find El Cacique viejo.

The afternoon grew hot as they trudged up the canyon through the Pinon and Juniper scrub. By late afternoon they had reached a transition area where Ponderosa and White Fir began to replace the scrub vegetation. The air began to cool down, too, and by twilight they had found a pleasant camp site in a small grove of aspens.

A tiny spring bubbled out of a rocky outcrop in the aspen grove and this fresh water made the after dinner tea delicious. Jed and Lucy talked quietly in the cool darkness as a three quarter moon rose over the Chuskas and lightning over the Defiance Plateau punctuated the beauty. Sleep gradually overtook them and the world of dreams was theirs, for awhile, again.

Morning found Jed pouring over USGS quad maps of the area and adjusting his compass. Lucy fixed a hearty breakfast of pancakes and coffee. By eight o'clock they were on their way north with plans to cut across the top end of several canyons looking for pot shards or any other sign that a pueblo might be located in the cliffs upstream.

Progress was slow and the terrain difficult. Both Lucy and Jed were caked with sweat and dust by noon and they had made very little progress. They were crossing the headwaters drainages of the Canyon de Chelly and the Little Colorado River, where some of the best cliff house pueblos in the southwest are. Here in the high country though, they were finding no sign of habitation.

By late afternoon they had made less than six miles and they were both exhausted. Jed made his way to the head of a small canyon and found a spring just below the rim rock. Jed suggested they set up camp for the night on the smooth slick rock above the spring and Lucy offered no argument.

After dinner that evening and before they crawled into their sleeping bags Lucy and Jed watched the light show from a major thunderstorm off to the southwest. They were not the only watchers that evening. Their arrival had been noticed and their activities had been closely observed by a strange and lonely inhabitant of this wild country.

Hidden in the rocks above the campsite, a Navajo witch watched like a predator. She was an ancient old hag clothed in skins of stolen goats. She was filthy and absolutely crazy from years of living alone in the canyon country. Local people knew about her and feared her. It was said she scavenged dead bodies from the places where traditional Navajos had gone to die and that she kept the putrid corpses in her cave where she copulated with them. She was fearful all right and dirty and very interested in the couple that lay on the slickrock below her.

Jed and Lucy were asleep early that evening. They were bone weary from the day's walk and they scarcely stirred as the thunder from the approaching storm grew louder. The wind began to blow harder and the unmistakable smell of rain filled the air.

Suddenly a bolt of lightning reached out from the clouds and struck a huge Ponderosa Pine just above the slickrock. The immediate and deafening crash of thunder caused Jed and Lucy to sit up quickly in their sleeping bags.

"Jesus H. Christ!" Jed shouted. "That was close!"

"The rain's about to hit," Lucy said getting out of her bag. "We better get the tarp over us."

Jed and Lucy spread the blue nylon tarp over their sleeping bags, weighted down the edges with stones and propped up the middle with their backpacks. They crawled under the tarp and back to their bags just as the first heavy rain drops began to fall.

It quickly became hot under the tarp and they lay there together on top of their sleeping bags listening to the steadily increasing frequency of rain drops hitting their crude shelter. As the noise increased Jed realized there would be no going back to sleep until the storm passed. He decided to pursue another course of action.

He reached over to Lucy who was lying on her back wearing only a snap buttoned flannel shirt. As the lightning flashed he carefully unsnapped the shirt and found a breast to hold. At every flash of lightning he could see Lucy illuminated for a moment in the strange blue light. She was smiling, and he continued his exploration.

He pulled himself closer and began to kiss the soft curve of the underside of her breast as he moved his hand to the inside of her thigh and across her sparse Navajo pubic hair. He felt her dark nipples rise to attention as he kissed them gently. Parts of him had come to rigid attention as well and as the storm raged above them he mounted her and to the accompaniment of the cumulonimbus symphony they danced the familiar but always different dance of love.

As the lovers reached their zenith so too it seemed did the storm. Jed rolled over on his back and lay there puffing like a locomotive as lightning flashed and thunder crashed incessantly.

Suddenly between lightning flashes the tarp was ripped away. Lucy and Jed both stood up in the driving rain. Jed felt for his backpack to find a flashlight. As usual in this time of greatest need he couldn't remember where he had packed it. In the next flash of lightning Jed saw Lucy standing and shivering with her arms tightly wrapped around herself.

Behind her Jed saw something that caused him to gasp. It was some sort of grimy fur clad apparition standing just a step or two behind Lucy and holding the tarp. Jed forgot the flashlight and stood up shouting at Lucy. His voice was drowned out by the wind and thunder but he thought he heard Lucy scream. He reached out for where he had last seen her but she was not there.

In the next flash he saw for one frightening instant a scene that made his blood run cold. The filthy fur clad thing was sitting astride a scrawny horse with a long tarp covered bundle lying across the withers. Jed ran toward the horse in the darkness but as the next flash illuminated the scene he saw nothing but trees and rock and mud.

Jed's mind was racing. For a few moments he could not think of what to do. Finally a measure of reason returned and he quickly found his flashlight, his boots and a slicker. As soon as he was prepared he started looking for tracks. In only a few minutes he found fresh unshod horse tracks in the mud at the edge of the slickrock.

As he followed the tracks down a seldom used trail, through the ponderosa woods, the storm began to diminish. Jed ran along following the trail as fast as he could. He was moving so rapidly that he almost did not notice that the trail dropped over a small canyon through a crevice in the rim rock.

Fortunately for Jed the three quarter moon reappeared just before he ran headlong over the cliff. He stopped suddenly as he sensed the drop off and as he stood on the canyon rim breathing hard he noticed a light coming from behind some rocks across the drainage. He studied the light carefully as his breath returned to normal. It was the flickering light of a fire filtering through the breakdown boulders that hid the entry to a rock shelter. Jed turned off his flashlight and put it in his slicker pocket. There was ample light now from the moon to find his way along the trail through the rim rock to the shelter.

As Jed crept nearer to the rock shelter he began to hear the insane cackling of a mad woman. He saw the wretched horse he had seen back at the camp tied to a dead juniper in the jumble of boulders outside the rock shelter.

Jed moved to within 100 feet of the shelter and hid behind a boulder. He could not believe what he saw inside. Lucy was tied by the hands and feet to a hide stretching frame, the wretched old woman in goat skins held a rusty butcher knife to her breast.

Lucy was splattered with mud and looked to be in shock. The old woman muttered incomprehensibly and poked at Lucy with one grimy hand while she raked the flat sides of the knife back and forth over Lucy's breast with the other.

Jed did not know what to do. He was afraid that if he rushed in to the rock shelter the witch would kill Lucy and he was equally afraid that the same would happen if he didn't. As he sat crouched behind the rock trying to decide what to do he was amazed to see a pack of coyotes running through the boulders toward the shelter.

The coyotes ran right into the witches lair and she turned to see what was happening. She slashed vainly at the nimble canines who pulled her away from Lucy. Once the coyotes had the witch safely away from Lucy they began to run in rapid circles around her. The witch seemed greatly disoriented by this and she eventually fell to the ground.

At that the coyotes fell upon her and began to consume her with great haste. The coyotes quickly reduced the witch to bones and as quickly as they appeared they vanished into the rocks yipping and farting as they ran.

Jed ran past the bones of the old woman and grabbed the butcher knife. He quickly cut the bindings from Lucy's feet and arms and wrapped her in his slicker. He propped her up against the wall of the rock shelter and began to check her for injuries. She was at first only semi-conscious but soon she began to moan and scream. Jed tried to comfort her as much as he could. He held her in his arms and rocked her gently.

Lucy finally began to cry and sob deeply. "Jed . . . what is going on? Who was that old woman?"

"I don't know," Jed answered. "A very crazy woman who is dead now." Jed looked at the pile of bones and shook his head in disbelief.

Suddenly they were both shocked to hear another human voice.

"Is she going to be all right?" Someone asked from the shadows of the boulders outside the rock shelter.

Jed quickly stood up to meet what he feared could be another threat. He was surprised and relieved to see the old cacique from his peyote vision emerge from the rocks.

"You're . . .you're . . . uhhh."

"Yes," the old man answered. "You can call me Pajarito or Paja for short. I'm sorry about the witch. She's been a problem for a long time around here. She'll harm no one in this world again. Will you be all right sister?"

Lucy looked at the cacique in disbelief and finally answered, "Yea, I guess I'll make it. Who the hell are you anyway? Who was the old lady? What is going on?"

Pajarito smiled and answered, "I am Pajarito, cacique to the thin stone builders when I first lived upon this earth. Now I am a cloud, the wind, a coyote, or again a cacique. Your man here has asked the creators to help him heal the earth where it has been gravely injured. I will try to help him to do that. Along this path we will walk there will be many dangers, some of them like this."

He pointed to the pile of bones.

"You have a love bond to this man," he continued, "and because of that you will share this path with him. I do not know if we can succeed in this quest. The forces contrary to the path of heart have grown powerful and dominant on this earth. I told your man to find me in the physical world and he has. Here in this canyon is where I made medicine when I first lived on the earth as a man. Now the ruin of my cliff house is where the coyote brothers live. They are your friends though it may not always seem so. They will help us in this quest as they have helped you here tonight. Go on back to your home now young warrior and live your life normally. Love this woman and work on clearing your mind of any bad thoughts, even for the people who poisoned the land around Tsoodzix. I will visit you again when the time is right and we will proceed on the quest. Do not anticipate me. Only live well and right and when you least expect it I will be there."

The old cacique, "Pajarito", turned and walked back into the rocks and vanished. Jed and Lucy sat quietly for a long while before finally agreeing that it was time to return to their camp.

Dawn was lighting the eastern sky as they made their way back across the canyon. As they climbed out on the rim rock a pack of coyotes began to yip and howl across the canyon. When he turned to look Jed recognized in the growing light the spire of rock near the head of the canyon and the cliff house ruin where he had first seen Pajarito. He knew then that by the strange series of events just ended he had fulfilled the instructions from the peyote vision.

Jed and Lucy walked back to camp slowly. She was barefoot and wearing only his slicker and he was naked except for his walking boots. The strange looking pair held each other as they made their way slowly back down the muddy path. They were weary, tired, and somewhat bewildered by the events of the night but more than anything they were glad to be alive and together.

They ate a soggy breakfast and dried out their clothes and gear over a pinon fire then made their way slowly back down the mountain to Jed's truck. The ride back to Santa Fe was quiet. Both of them were tired and reflective. Before they got to Grants, Lucy was asleep with her head in Jed's lap.

Jed watched the darkness swallow up the sacred mountain as he drove on toward Albuquerque. He watched it in his rear view mirror and wondered if he would ever see it erupt. They pulled into Jed's driveway by 11:30 PM and both were sound asleep before midnight.

Up in the mountains above town, 12,000 feet up in the cool Sangre de Cristos, there in the clear moonlight with his foot on the Lake Peak bench mark was Pajarito. The ancient, ageless, timeless cacique watched the flickering lights of Santa Fe and smiled. He knew the young warrior was there in the middle of the crystal blanket that was this ancient city at the foot of the mountains. There entangled with his lover, heir to the aboriginal spirit, dreaming of the dreamer dreaming of the dream.

There was much ground to cover if that sacred mountain there just beyond the harsh glare of Albuquerque was to remake a bit of the world. Yes there was much to do, and much more to dream.

❖

CHAPTER VI-SUMMER GROWTH

Lucy and Jed slipped into a warm New Mexico summer with ease. Most days were spent together wandering the high country and enjoying each other's company. Occasionally Jed had to turn his attention to a contract obligation but even on extended field surveys Lucy was usually there.

For a week in July Lucy took the bus back to Torreon and spent some time with her aging grandparents. Jed felt her absence like the loss of an appendage. He had grown ever deeper in love with his Navajo beauty and she with him since their reunion in the spring. He eagerly awaited her return and had planned a pack trip to the Pecos Wilderness to celebrate the reunion.

Two days before Lucy returned Jed was walking at twilight along the Acequia Madre in his neighborhood. He was comfortable here. He knew everyone in almost every house. The sound of the water in the ditch and the wind in the cottonwoods was familiar and soothing. This was Jed's home turf, he knew it well and felt secure in the belief that nothing could surprise him here.

Jed's confident security was shaken when he heard a strangely familiar voice call out over his left shoulder. "Take my hand young warrior. I want to show you some things you have never seen."

Jed spun around on his boot heels and saw the old cacique Pajarito in a velveteen shirt and Levis.

"Where did you come from?"

"Just now . . . or originally?" The old man asked with a smile.

Jed just looked at the cacique and blinked.

"Right now, " Pajarito continued in a moment, "I've come directly from the place I just was . . . which cannot be adequately descibed in spoken words. That's why I want you to take my hand and come with me to this unspeakable place where your measure of time and distance have no meaning. Here now . . . take my hand."

Jed looked for a few long moments at the ancient outstretched hand before him then without further hesitation he pressed his own palm to Pajarito's.

"There now," Pajarito assured Jed. "This is that place you asked about."

Jed looked around at the familiar scenery of his neighborhood then looked at Pajarito. "I don't understand. This is where I live. I see it every day. Nothing is different."

"It may look the same to you," the old man said looking into Jed's eyes. "But you don't look the same to it. In fact no one in this neighborhood can see you . . . except maybe a few very sensitive dogs."

"How can that be?" Jed asked. "It all looks exactly like my every day reality. How can I not be part of it?"

"Of course you are a part of it," Pajarito answered. "You're just operating at a different frequency right now and almost no one at your normal frequency can tell in any way that you are here. We don't need these surroundings, but I thought you would be more confortable at first in a familiar setting."

"What do you mean, at first?" Jed asked scratching the side of his face. "Where are we going? What's going to happen?"

"Don't fear young warrior . . . never, never, never fear anything . . . really . . . its very important for what we are going to be doing . . . today and in the future . . . if you are still certain about this quest. If you are, and I think you are, then today we can go as far and do as much as you wish. Nothing more, nothing less. So what will it be . . . anything, really almost absolutely anything is possible when you get beyond the chains of three dimensions."

Jed looked thoughtful for a while then smiled weakly. "Well you know . . . I really liked the feeling of stepping off the rock spire where your kiva was in my peyote vision, and walking on those stepping stones through the air."

"Fine!" Pajarito said. "We can start that way . . . but let's dispense with the stepping stones and just walk on into what you see as the airspace above your world."

Pajarito pulled Jed's hand gently and took a step into the air. Jed followed, and in a few minutes they were both strolling above the cottonwoods and light poles. The two men walked slowly across the Paseo and over the gardens of the state capital building. Jed laughed when he saw from this unique vantage point the fashion show and pretentious flirtation of the open air patrons of Patisse Korbae. In a short while the air hikers were over the plaza and Jed could easily see two young theives breaking into a car parked behind the Ore House and on the roof of the Patron building he saw the heir to this empire of political theives, Norville Patron rubbing oil on his legal secretary's buttocks.

Jed was content to amuse himself with a treetop level tour of his hometown for a considerable period before he finally looked up to the mountains above town and had another thought. "Hey, I'm going up there on horses in a few days . . . it would sure be cool if we could go up there like this."

"And so we shall," Pajarito said with a twinkle in his eye, and in an instant they were there hovering over Santa Fe Baldy.

"Wow!" Jed howled. "What a trip! I can just be anywhere by thinking it . . . is that the deal?"

"Thats pretty much the deal," Pajarito answered.

Jed looked across the Rio Grande Valley at Santa Clara Peak in the Jemez Mountains and thought, "I want to be there." In another instant he was.

"Now young warrior," Pajarito spoke after a few moments in a low voice, "it is true, we could be anywhere in an instant and we could probably be very amused by it for a long while, but that is not the point to be made here and now. This is just one way to introduce you to the concept of multiple realities. For over a thousand of your three dimensional years I have explored a tiny bit of the infinite. When I need to, I exist and operate quite well in your place and time . . . but the power to affect the great forces of three dimensional reality by force of individual will comes from far beyond the confines of your world. I am not the only explorer of the infinite . . . there are many others from many places. I am, though, your principle guide to the power of the infinite. It will be my task to point to the places you must go to learn the dance you must know if you are to affect the mighty forces of this planet's nature. Two things must be learned first before we can go farther. You must not fall into the trap of intellectual inquiry. How all this works is not nearly as important as accepting without question that it does. Also you must avoid the abyss of fear. You will see and hear things that could kill a man who allows fear to grip his heart. You must learn to live without fear and without question of the power you will soon be feeling. Now . . .you are back where we first met today and not an instant of your time has been lost."

And so it was that Jed was back walking along the acequia alone again listening to the murmurring of the wind and the water. He stopped for a moment, shook his head and rubbed his eyes then continued on his walk. For the next twenty four hours or so Jed felt as though he was in a fog, a strange half dream state that only began to clear up as his anticipation of Lucy's arrival heightened.

When Jed met Lucy at the bus station he was prepared to drive out on the Caja del Rio and spend the night under the stars. He had every sleeping bag and blanket he owned piled in the back of his pickup so they could sleep in the truckbed away from the rattlesnakes and tarantulas. He also had a cooler full of ice surrounding two bottles of Lucy's favorite wine.

Jed was ready and he knew it. As he rumbled out of town with his love beside him he was smiling the smile of a man who was about to indulge in the most satisfying and fulfilling of endeavors in which a man could engage.

The night was brilliant and lighted perfectly by a quarter moon. The coyotes sang and the owls hooted as two lovers renewed their bond.

As dawn streaked the sky above the Sangre de Cristo Mountains Lucy sat up in the truck and watched a wild horse herd move across the plateau toward the Rio Grande. She looked down at the man still sleeping beside her and softly said, "Thank you Grandfathers for this man here who loves me. Help him to be a warrior and fight the good battle for the sacred mountain."

Jed stirred and rolled over, opened one eye and asked, "Is this today?"

"All day hostene." Lucy answered brushing the hair from his face.

After breakfast burritos they headed for Jed's place and on the way he explained the plan for the pack trip to the Pecos Wilderness. Jed had arranged for three horses to be trailered up from Terrero to Jack's Creek by an outfitter friend of his. From there he planned to ride up past the Pecos Baldys and on into the Truchas Peaks for a few days of montaine splender, then back by way of Rito Padre and Beatty's Cabin through Iron Gate and back to Jack's Creek.

The plan sounded fine to Lucy who had never been to the Pecos country and they were set to head out the following morning.

The cool of the evening moved them to migrate down the Old Santa Fe Trail to the Plaza. Jed had margaritas on his mind and Lucy was hungry as usual. Both needs could be fulfilled at La Fonda, the old inn at the end of the Santa Fe Trail.

As usual La Fonda was full of people who looked like they had just walked in from a movie set. Some of them no doubt had. There were the requisite crystal clean cowboys with turquoise scarves and a few Indians straight from central casting. There were also a number of green and purple spiked heads just for spice.

Seated at the piano was a robust black female blues singer in a sequined gown and a huge foam rubber imitation fruit basket hat. She was belting out Pearl Baileyesque songs with gusto and downing dry martinis between bawdy jokes.

Lucy and Jed found a small table in a dimly lit corner of the bar room. In a few minutes a pretty young Spanish waitress appeared and took their order. She was wearing a pleated blue fiesta dress and a cotton Mexican blouse that had slipped off of one shoulder.

When she turned toward Lucy to take her order Jed noticed her tattoo exposed by the drooping sleeve. It was the familiar Virgin of Guadalupe and underneath it accentuated by a dagger dripping blood was the name, "Ramon." Jed was still smiling at the body art when he gave her his order.

"Margarita on the rocks, no salt and put it in a beer glass not a bird bath." She nodded and scampered off toward the bar.

Lucy reached out and took Jed's hand and smiled at him. "Its good to be with you again hostene," she said smiling.

Jed sighed and leaned back against the irregular stucco wall. "I missed you Lucy. Its gonna be real hard when you go back to school."

Lucy lost her smile and looked up at the latillas on the ceiling. "I know Jed. I've been thinking about that. I've gotten real used to you being beside me at night. I have a hard time sleeping without you." She smiled again as their drinks arrived along with her nachos.

"Well babe," Jed said with a grin as he lifted his glass. "Here's to right now when we are together. Let's make the best of it."

They clicked their glasses and drank.

As the two lovers stared at each others eyes in the dark quiet corner of the bar they heard a commotion in the lobby. Someone with a heavy Texas accent was shouting.

"Hold open them doors, honey. I'm a comin' through."

They heard the revving of a motorcycle engine and in a moment they saw a man wearing nothing but red boxer shorts, lizard skin boots and an oversized Stetson come roaring into the hotel lobby on a Harley Davidson 883cc Sportster. He paused for a minute and smiled at the dazed desk clerk, tipped his hat and drove his machine somehow up the curving steps to the mezzanine balcony overlooking the restaurant.

Within a few seconds the turban headed Acme security force was on the scene. "Where did he go?" one of them shouted at the desk clerk who seemed by now to be in shock. He could not answer but their query was resolved by the sound of the crazed cyclist roaring around the mezzanine balcony singing "I fought the law but the law won."

When the Acme men appeared at the top of the winding stairs, the maniac cowboy biker halted at the far end of the balcony and considered his options, occasionally goosing the throttle of his Harley. He pushed his hat back on his head and stared at the turbaned security men, and with a puzzled look he asked, "How come ya'll are wearin' them diapers on your heads? Ya'll some kind of Arabs or somethin'?" He grinned, but they did not. The Acme men pulled their night sticks from their utility belts and began to close in on him.

The mechanical cowboy began to feel trapped, hemmed in, corralled. His options were limited. He could make a dash for it down one side or the other of the mezzanine balcony but even in his seriously inebriated state he realized one of those night sticks would find its mark on his head and his free riding days would be over. No, there had to be another way. The Acme men were getting closer and they did not seem amused by the situation.

Then it came to him. The answer was right before his eyes. During one of his circuits of the balcony he had knocked over a heavy wooden coffee table and it was now positioned with one end over the balcony rail and the other nearly touching the floor. A ramp, if you will.

His ticket back to Dallas, and freedom, and all that goes with that notion, lay before him if only he were crazy enough to try it. He grinned and walked his machine backward until he hit the wall opposite the ramp. He pulled his hat on securely, revved his engine, popped the clutch, and managed to hit second gear just before leaving the ramp and becoming airborne. He cut with a rebel yell as he descended into the airspace of the now fortunately deserted dining room. He landed on the tile floor barely missing two tables and roared on through the lobby.

He almost slid past an elegantly dressed woman as she pushed open the heavy double doors to the hotel entry corridor. Unfortunately, for her, his shifter peg snagged the bottom of her loose, slinky silk evening dress and as he proceeded down the corridor her dress was ripped from her body in a most un-dignified fashion. As the maniac roared out of the hotel and on to San Francisco Street, a gust of wind blew his hat off and it sat there in the middle of the street like his calling card.

In a few moments the Acme men and the Santa Fe Police arrived at the hotel entrance but were mainly involving themselves in comforting the poor naked lady this beast had disrobed. As the defenders of justice stood in a tight little group protecting the virtues of womanhood the crazed perpetrator of the crime appeared again.

This time he was moving at a high rate of speed in the wrong direction down the one way street where his hat lay quietly on the pavement. He reached down and retrieved his hat as he passed it, and whooping like a banshee he headed out of town, at a high rate of speed.

The police were beside themselves, not being sure whether they should continue to protect the naked lady or roar off in pursuit of the criminal. Radios crackled and sirens wailed all over the city, but off south of town a cowboy in boxer shorts was smiling and moving out across the plains toward Texas at nearly 100 miles per hour, and nothing short of an empty gas tank could stop him.

Now that the initial shock was over, Jed and Lucy were bowed over with laughter in the bar. It had been a fine night of cheap entertainment and as the police questioned witnesses Jed and Lucy slipped out the side door and walked on home laughing all the way.

Jed made sure all his camping gear was ready to pack in the panniers the next day. He was excited about introducing Lucy to his beloved Pecos Wilderness.

The Pecos River Canyon was beautiful in the early morning light as Jed and Lucy wound their way up the narrow road. The pavement ends at the

Terrero Store and it was there that Jed stopped to load the horses and tack. His outfitter friend had already caught up the three horses Jed needed and in only a few minutes the little caravan was headed slowly on up the dusty road to Jack's Creek. The narrow dirt track from Terrero to the edge of the wilderness passed through uniformly magnificent country with the exception of the obscene mine dumps along Willow creek. It took nearly 40 minutes to cover the few miles to Jack's creek. Saddling up and packing the panniers took another 30 minutes but by nine o'clock Lucy and Jed were riding through the cool forest on the trail to Round Mountain.

The high country air was always intoxicating to Jed. The crisp clarity of the vistas and the friendly comfort of the mixed conifers and aspens always felt like coming home. The horses knew the trail by heart and there was no need to guide them. This gave the riders plenty of latitude to sight-see and talk. Lucy looked radiant in her long wrapped braids and faded Levi's jacket. Her voice was like music that blended well with the calls of camp-robbers and stellars jays.

A mile before Round Mountain the forest gave way to great sub-alpine meadows punctuated with little groves of aspen and stands of Bristlecone Pine. Riding in the open meadow country it soon became quite warm and Lucy took off her jacket and tied it behind her saddle. Jed thought she looked magnificent in her purple tank top shirt with her unconfined breasts moving gently under the cotton cloth. He thought once again, as he did so often these days, of what a lucky man he was, indeed.

At the north end of Round Mountain the trail dropped back into the Engleman Spruce again and soon crossed Jack's Creek for the first time since the trailhead. Jed stopped the horses in the middle of the stream and let them drink their fill. He pulled a slab of carne seca from his saddle bags and offered it to Lucy.

She shook her head and answered, "No thanks. I'm waiting till we get to the Dairy Queen."

Jed grunted and smiled as he pulled the pack horse back up on to the trail and headed into the dark Engleman forest again. The next few miles were through the cool, dark, enclosed world of old growth spruce. Finally the trees began to thin out and a massive conical peak appeared. As they rode in to the glacial circ in front of East Pecos Baldy they saw the great peak reflected in the deep blue mirror of Pecos Lake. A female Big Horn Sheep and her young of the year were drinking at the water's edge. They looked up at the intruders for only a moment before continuing their drink.

Lucy and Jed made their way up a series of switch backs and through a deep snow bank to the 12,000 foot crest of the ridge known as Trailrider's

Wall. There they rested the horses again and gazed directly into the 13,000 foot Truchas Peaks.

Jed explained to Lucy that the high ridge they were on had been an important hunting camp several thousand years ago to a mysterious people that archaeologists knew very little about. He pointed out the obsidian chips on the ground where ancient hunters had crafted tools of this volcanic glass from the Jemez Mountains clearly visible across the Rio Grande valley 40 miles to the west.

The expected afternoon thunderheads were already building off to the southwest as they rode across the ridge and into the patchy forest under the Truchas Peaks. The trail from that point into the Truchas Lakes was steep and rocky and the pace of the horses was accordingly reduced. It was late afternoon before Jed found his chosen campsite in a small meadow below the lakes. There was a spring in the meadow and a great view of middle and south Truchas peaks.

Jed set about erecting the tent as thunder rumbled beyond the peaks. Lucy gathered dead limbs from spruce trees and soon had a great warming fire going. The sun was behind the peaks before their bean and rice dinner was ready. It became very cool as they ate and both of them were ready for the relative warmth of the tent soon after dinner. Jed checked the picketed horses one more time before joining Lucy in the tent. The two lovers created considerable warmth in their shelter before drifting into sound sleep in each others arms.

The threatening thunderstorms finally arrived shortly before midnight. The sound of the thunder and heavy rain were deafening but at one point Jed thought he heard the horses. He reluctantly got up, found his slicker, pulled on his boots and went out to make sure they were all right. They seemed scared by the lighting but otherwise OK and still secure on their picket line.

Jed was just about to enter the tent again when a close strike of lightning turned his head. To his amazement he saw in the brief flash the figure of a man standing on the high ridge above camp with his arms outstretched to the violent sky. Jed stood in the darkness after the flash and thought that anyone crazy enough to be up there in a thunderstorm must have a serious death wish. In a few seconds another great flash illuminated the figure again. This time Jed felt strangely that somehow this person was calling to him.

He was suddenly gripped with paralyzing fear. Lightning continued to strike the peaks and the ridge all around this strange person. Jed wanted to go back into the tent and lie with Lucy and forget this crazy individual on the ridge but another part of him was moved to investigate.

Against his better judgment and all the mountain sensibilities he had developed over the years Jed began to climb toward the figure on the ridge.

Once he ascended above the trees he was on a rough scree slope that often gave way under his steps. With each new flash of lightning he could see the figure a little better. He could tell now that it was a man. He seemed to be singing and dancing and generally enjoying the dangerous pyrotechnics around him.

Jed's fear had given way to wonder and curiosity. He finally reached the ridge about 200 feet south of where this wild dancer performed. As he approached the man he saw a strange blue glow develop over South Truchas Peak. This odd blue light was undulating and crackling over the peak like static electricity on a wool blanket in winter. Suddenly and with an ominous rumble the blue light coalesced into a large ball and began to roll down the ridge toward the dancer and Jed.

Jed watched with a strange sense of wonder as the beautiful, but no doubt deadly, ball lightning bore down upon him. At the last possible moment the mysterious dancer leapt high into the air, higher it seemed than was humanly possible and the rolling electrical apparition proceeded beneath him toward Jed.

Jed realized, perhaps a little too late, that he was in quite a bad position. He could not possibly run fast enough off the ridge to escape the blue dynamo bearing down on him. As he stood there watching with strange fascination he accepted with relative ease what he took to be his certain and unavoidable death. With this acceptance a pervasive sense of calm overtook him and he smiled passively. Within a few feet of Jed and with a great peal of thunder the ball lightning fell apart and slithered down the ridge like a hundred electric serpents.

Jed was charged, electrically for sure, but also in spirit. This calm facing of his death and banishment of fear was therapeutic and uplifting. As Jed stood revelling in his present state of mind and heart, he was jolted by a human voice.

"Very good young warrior. You have beaten the demon of fear. Man's worst enemy."

Jed turned his eyes toward the voice and saw the smiling face of Pajarito. He laughed and said, "Well, I'm not even surprised. Do you often dance with lightning?"

"Yes!" Pajarito answered. "Its my second favorite thing to do in the physical realm."

Distant lightning continued to flash over the Pecos country as Jed and Pajarito stood on the ridge together. Jed's eyes were drawn to the tent in the meadow below.

"I better get back down there. Lucy will be worried if she wakes up."

"Yes," Pajarito said with a nod. "Go on back now, you've learned this lesson well. There are more to learn . . . later. For now go on back to your woman and engage in my favorite activity in the physical realm."

Jed watched silently for a few minutes as Pajarito walked slowly up the ridge toward South Truchas Peak singing a soft little Pueblo song. Finally he made his way carefully over the scree slope back to camp and the warmth and comfort of Lucy's body.

Jed was sleeping like a dead man when dawn crept over the mountains. Lucy was awakened by the jays and ravens and increasing light. She could tell by Jed's breathing that he was sound asleep and needed to be. She slipped out of the tent and silently rekindled the fire. She sat beside it warming herself and watched the changing light on the peaks. She built a pot of strong Navajo style coffee and put it in the edge of the small fire. The smell of that, combined with the growing warmth of the day, finally roused Jed.

After an ample breakfast, Jed prepared the horses while Lucy broke camp. By mid-morning they were headed out of the Truchas country and toward Chimayosos Peak. The sky was crystalline cobalt and the wind was like the breath of a mouse. It was hard for either of them to imagine a more perfect morning or a more perfect place to enjoy it.

The view from the gap just west of Chimayosos was of high timberline peaks in all directions. They stayed on the high trail toward Santa Barbara Peak for a mile or so before dropping off into the spruce forest around the headwaters of Rito Padre.

The trail through the thick woods was often blocked by blowdowns and their progress was slow. By mid afternoon when they finally stopped for lunch the horses were lathered and bleeding from a few minor cuts around their ankles caused by broken branches in the blowdowns. The trail conditions did not improve appreciably until they were well down into the Padre drainage.

By late afternoon when camp was established in the meadows near the confluence of Rito Padre and the Pecos River both horses and riders were very tired campers. The requisite evening thunderstorms were scarcely noticed by Jed and Lucy as they slept in their customary embrace. Once again Jed heard the horses complaining about the weather but this time he did not check on them. He halfway feared what he might see standing on the grassy hill above camp dancing in the storm. He pulled his sleeping bag over his head, hugged Lucy, and returned to the world of dreams.

The next morning it was still raining. No thunder or lightning, just a steady cold rain. Breakfast was short and sweet and in the tent before Jed pulled on his slicker and proceeded with the morning ritual of readying the horses.

Pulling up the trail through the woods back to Round Mountain was a soggy muddy mess of a ride. By the time they reached the big meadows the cold rain had turned to snow corn blowing in biting and stinging sheets across the ridge.

Lucy, who had wrapped herself in a Mexican blanket, rode up to Jed and asked, "Are we still having fun, hostene?"

Jed wiped the ice away from his eye brows and looked at Lucy. "No," he answered quietly. "We're not having fun any more."

Lucy blew on her half frozen fingers. "You know Jed . . . the sun is probably shining down in Santa Fe. We could be lying naked somewhere on a warm rock."

Jed sniffed and shook the snow pellets from his slicker sleeve. "All right," he said feigning disgust. "I can't counter a suggestion like that. Follow me." With his back safety turned toward Lucy, Jed smiled broadly and headed down the ridge toward Jack's Creek and home.

They rode out of the cold rain and back into brilliant sunshine before they got to the Jack's creek campground. Things were pretty well dried out by the time they reached the truck. They loaded all the gear and the saddle from Lucy's horse into the pickup and Lucy slowly drove Jed's old Willys down the road to Terrero while Jed rode and led the two other horses. It was late afternoon before Jed and Lucy had returned the borrowed mounts, put away the gear, and spent a decent amount of time talking and drinking beer with Jed's friends at the Terrero store.

It was indeed warm and sunny in Santa Fe and although it was a little late to find a warm rock to lie naked on Jed thought of a reasonable and more comfortable facsimile at his house and Lucy was easily talked into the substitution.

The next few weeks were spent in an easy combination of work and play that kept Jed in funds and Lucy well fed and happy. As the end of summer crept closer, Jed decided there needed to be one more good outing together before Lucy returned to school.

He had been hearing about a big end of summer celebration planned for late August in the wild little Colorado mountain town of Telluride. The high point of the celebration was to be a huge outdoor Grateful Dead concert. Normally, Jed was not drawn to big crowd events but there was something about this one that attracted him. Lucy liked the idea as she had never before seen a big outdoor rock 'n roll show and neither had she been to Telluride. Both seemed like wild and dangerous enticements and she was ready for a new type of adventure.

Jed packed all the necessary camping gear and supplies in his truck the night before their departure. At dawn on a clear and still late August morning they headed out for Telluride.

The drive to Telluride from Santa Fe is almost as interesting as any adventure that might occur in one or the other of these free zone cities. Jed chose the mountain route for the trip up. It carried them through Chama, Pagosa Springs, Durango, Silverton, and Ouray. Jed stopped at Red Mountain Pass to fill his ice chest with snow that had never quite melted from the past winter. This was also a point on the continental divide and of course Jed could not resist a urinary contribution to North America's great river systems. Lucy laughed until she ached then realized she too needed to relieve herself. Jed cajoled her into also dividing her contribution along the continental backbone. They both discovered that like many things in life, men have an easier time than women, but with diligence, accomplished bladder control, and fancy pants around the knees footwork they were able to assure a fair contribution to both edges of the continent.

By the time they pulled into Telluride, the little town had been taken over by a peaceful invasion of colorful Deadheads. A carnival atmosphere prevailed as they made their way through the city center and up a dirt road that ascended the south facing slope of the narrow glacial valley above Telluride. Jed four wheeled his way into the center of a grove of aspens and proceeded to set up a camp in a small meadow with a view of the town below.

As the late afternoon color began to deepen, Lucy and Jed walked down the dirt road into town. The tie dyed army was in firm but peaceful control of every street. Minstrels and jugglers entertained young and old. Primitive rhythms filled the night air and smiles were endemic and infectious among the multitudes.

The town police were pleasantly reminding people that glass containers were not welcome on the streets while at the same time they seemed not at all concerned about the growing cloud of sweet illegal smoke engulfing the little village. The colorful invaders complied passively with the simple rules of the free zone and peace and happiness set the tone for the next two days of revelry.

Jed and Lucy elbowed their way into a very crowded saloon and with some persistence managed to obtain two margaritas. They saw a small space of wall against which they could lean and watch the show. And quite a show it was. Several minstrels were playing everything from banjos to pan pipes in different parts of the saloon. People were dancing and singing in total oblivion to all the rules and constraints that prevailed outside of this temporarily liberated space. In one corner of the saloon leg wrestling was the dominant activity and the entangled limbs of participants in this endeavor were the cause of many cheers and much laughter.

At one point a magnificently beautiful young woman with long wavy brown hair and a white cotton see through dress climbed onto the bar and began to dance while clicking little finger cymbals. Every heterosexual male eye in the room including Jed's was riveted to this slinky undulating female form. Lucy, however, was watching Jed watching this freeform exhibitionist and her ire was rising with each passing moment.

Finally Lucy could stand it no longer and she tapped Jed on the shoulder and as he turned toward her she said, "If you're so interested in mammaries how about these!"

With that she ripped open her flannel shirt revealing her own which provoked a round of cheers and applause. Jed turned up his drink, removed Lucy's from her hand, and finished it too, then smiled and said, "Time to go Lucy. Its past my bed time you know, and when I don't get my rest I get very cranky."

Jed led Lucy by the hand back through the frolicking multitudes and up the dirt road to their camp above town. Lucy giggled most of the way remembering the look on Jed's face when she ripped open her shirt.

Jed was quiet until they got back to the camp where he took Lucy in his arms and kissed her with feeling and clear intent to do more. "I love you Lucy," he whispered between kisses as he carefully removed her shirt.

Jed quickly pulled some blankets from his truck and spread them on the thick meadow grass. He then carefully placed Lucy on the ground and proceeded to remove the rest of her clothing. After disrobing himself he lay beside her and began to kiss her lips, then her breasts, then her stomach and thighs, and then everything from her toes northward. Her cries of delight mingled with the night sounds in the mountains and the stars were witness to the timeless human dance of passion that rose and fell like ocean tides throughout the night.

The next morning they slept as late as the brilliant sunlight and the growing murmur of human voices in the town below them would allow. Finally, one at a time, Lucy first of course, they joined the world of the awakened. Lucy whipped up a breakfast of pancakes and coffee and by late morning they were ready to join the celebrating multitudes.

They wore bright tie dyed tank tops purchased the previous day from itinerant Deadhead street merchants and cut off Levi's. Jed and Lucy were ready to dance and so apparently were 25,000 other similarly dressed individuals.

The carnival atmosphere was potent by the time they reached the occupied city. The air was charged with the kind of electricity that only the Grateful Dead could generate. This band of middle aged rockers had been spawning this sort of celebration for nearly 25 years and the energy had not dissipated a bit with the passage of time.

As usual at least half the show was the audience. No where else on earth on this particular day was quite such a colorful road show in progress. The cast of characters included ages ranging from new born to 80 years old. Everything from down and out street folks to millionaire yuppies all together all in their tie dyes all smiling and dancing and loving each other and life.

There was Bill Graham in his Boy Scout shorts and steal your face tee shirt. A rock and roll impresario magnifique on his Honda 250 smiling and checking out the crowd. Here was Hugh Romney, AKA Wavy Gravy, in full clown costume up from the Hog Farm in Llano, New Mexico. And there walking from shadow to shadow, like a lizard, was Ed Abbey in his favorite Colorado mountain town, "TO HELL YOU RIDE".

That was the big show. The people, the personalities and the humor. And up on the stage in the town park under the gently flapping tarps things were beginning to stir. Drums of all description were set up. Microphones were adjusted. Something was about to happen and the people felt it.

Lucy and Jed were smiling and walking around the tightly packed deadheads in front of the stage. The pirate tape makers were there too. A time honored Grateful Dead tradition fully supported by the band. The clandestine recording studio was set up squarely in the middle of the field in front of the stage. All was made ready for the celebration. Frisbees were flying, mothers were nursing their offspring, dogs were barking and fornicating, the sun was shining in a cloudless sky.

Jed recognized people now and then and they waived to one another. A wildly painted bus from New Mexico was parked to one side of the stage and Jed was observed and called over by the ragged band of gypsies standing in and around it. They proved to be a very friendly bunch and Lucy was very glad to meet them and accepted readily their offer of green chile burritos and fresh lemonade.

A fine time was had by all as joints were lit and offered and politely declined, by Lucy at least.

Then an announcer, none other than Bill Graham himself, stepped up to the microphone. He thanked everyone for coming, reminded them to clean up their trash and announced the opening act: Baba Olatunji and his drums of passion.

At that a wild African rhythm developed from the assemblage of drums and a parade of dancing women in native dress entered the stage from both sides. The huge crowd roared its approval and for a few moments the drums were drowned out by the shouts of the audience. Jed and Lucy finished off one more glass of lemonade and waived goodbye to their friends at the bus as they wandered back into the crowd.

The ragged gypsies waived back with a greeting, shouted in unison, "Have a nice trip!"

Jed turned back, suddenly aware of the significance of this greeting and looked at his smiling, waiving friends on the bus, then at Lucy who was smiling and moving to the jungle rhythms oblivious to the chemical chain reaction now underway in her brain.

With a sigh and a silent "Oh well", Jed too joined the undulating masses moving to the African beat.

Baba Olatunji and his 12 drums of passion and 20 dancing women entertained the crowd corralled between high mountains for nearly an hour before yielding to the headline band.

As the stage hands scurried under the flapping tarps Lucy and Jed began to notice some subtle but undeniable changes in sensory perception. Lucy began to feel that the gentle breeze that cooled her body was also blowing right through her. As she watched the stage she saw it, and everything else, begin to separate into several multicolored and slightly disconnected but identical layers. Her ears buzzed and her skin tingled. Jed, too, was feeling similar perceptual changes but he knew the cause. He turned to Lucy and tried to explain what had happened but words in the common sense would not form, only grunts and animal-like noises.

Lucy looked at Jed as he tried to speak and began to laugh. Her laughter seemed to be contagious and soon the mountains echoed with the wild laughter of thousands of people obviously in the same state of mind.

When the Grateful Dead finally walked on stage the crowd roared its approval and the first strains of music were obscured by the sound. Soon the vocal response gave way to motion. Dancing became the primary means of communication. Jed and Lucy joined the multitudes and danced completely through the two hour first set.

By the time the band took a rest both Jed and Lucy were soaring. Lucy had long since realized that the feeling and the phenomena were more than indigestion and she accepted her fate and made the best of it. Jed who had been in this particular state of mind before sensed Lucy's acceptance and also resigned himself to enjoying the show.

The day was dazzling and the company was good. The music was fine and all physical needs for the time were addressed. They had a fine time as they soared and whirled in the good company of fellow revelers.

Toward the end of the day and the concert Jed and Lucy became more accustomed to their state of being and began to enjoy some of the more colorful characters around them. No one dances quite like a deadhead and the variety of their dress was only exceeded by the originality of their movement. Everything from wild leaps and gymnastics to graceful rock ballet was involved in the motion around them.

It was not entirely lost on Lucy that Jed was drawn to the graceful form of one particular group of beautiful young women in flimsy cotton dresses. Their movement was indeed art in motion and even Lucy could see the beauty in their swirling bodies.

As Jed stood entranced watching them dance he saw what appeared to be an old man come cartwheeling in to their midst. The white haired acrobat was wearing faded Levis, a purple tie die t-shirt and a turquoise bandana around his head. Suddenly, this extremely agile old man did a multiple back flip and landed directly in front of Jed. Jed was amazed to see the smiling face of Pajarito resplendent in his deadhead outfit. Lucy too recognized the old cacique. Both she and Jed were dumbfounded.

Pajarito saw this and laughed.

"And what do you think the lesson of this day is?" he asked scratching his chin.

Lucy and Jed still could not talk.

"The lesson," he began to answer sensing he would get no response, "is that truth, beauty, happiness, and the key to other realms can be found down many paths. This is a ceremony every bit as valid and powerful as any ever held in a Great Kiva. These people are as much the keepers of primal tradition as any cacique or the Dali Lama. Sell nothing short in your search for the way. Walk down every path. Look under every stone. The truth is waiting for you. It is yours. The mountain can be made to bleed a new skin. The world can be new. You can be responsible for that happening but only with the help and participation of the collective force of all life. Its right here all around you. The kingdom of heaven really is right at hand. Right here. The answer really is blowing in the wind. Listen to it, pay attention, never give up. Keep searching young warrior and keep loving your lady. But right now keep on dancing."

With that Pajarito cartwheeled back into the crowd and out of sight but not out of mind.

The music faded with the days last light. The colorful deadhead multitudes flowed into the streets under a yet more colorful banket of southwestern twilight sky. Jed and Lucy flowed with the throng into the heart of the tiny mountain town and broke away from the mainstream of humanity at the courthouse.

They followed less crowded lanes and alleys between restored victorians and picket fences to a dirt track at the north edge of town. From there the old road took a steep track up the ridge above Telluride to several patented mining claims.

Lucy stopped at an ore loadout perched on the side of the mountain about 300' above town. She walked out onto a heavy beam that supported the ore cars on the loadout. Jed was a few steps ahead of Lucy and at first he didn't notice that she had stopped.

When he realized what Lucy was doing he wheeled around on his heels and shouted, "Lucy! Get off of there! That old piece of shit could fall down at any time."

"No," she answered slowly and softly. "Its not going to fall. Its so sturdy we could dance out here." She stomped her foot to emphasize the point and threw out her arms as she spun around toward the town below her.

"Come on Jed. Come on out here and dance with me."

Jed just shook his head.

Lucy took a deep breath and smiled. "Come on Jed," she said again in a whisper as she began to pull off her shirt.

Jed watched for a moment and his heart began to quicken. The stitching in the crotch of his faded Levis cutoffs tightened noticeably. She was still the most beautiful woman Jed had ever seen. When Lucy dropped her shirt and her breasts were free in the night air Jed could resist no longer. He stepped out onto the loadout beams and between shortened breaths tried to remove his clothes in transit. He stopped after nearly falling off the beam and carefully removed his garments as he watched Lucy do the same.

Jed and Lucy made love on the loadout above Telluride until well into the morning hours. As they reveled in each other the deadhead revelers below rocked the town in their own form of lovers embrace.

A pale light of dawn was showing before Jed and Lucy climbed on up to where their camp was setup in the aspen grove. After a midmorning breakfast the camp was broken and a quiet and orderly retreat was made from Telluride and the San Juan Mountains.

They headed south past Mesa Verde and Cortez and on into Farmington before stopping for fuel and food. Out of Farmington, Jed turned south onto the Bisti Road.

Out in the sea of wild desolation between Farmington and Crown Point, Lucy turned to Jed and spoke.

"You know Jed . . . I've been thinking about this crazy idea of yours about causing Mt. Taylor to erupt. After getting to know this little pueblo high priest friend of yours I'm beginning to believe that it just might be possible. And that scares me."

Jed raised his right hand and started to speak but Lucy interupted.

"No Jed. Hear me out. Not only do I think its dangerous to fuck around with Anazasi magic, I also think you've delegated Grants and all the other little

towns around Mt. Taylor to the status of the evil villages in the old legend."
"What do you mean?" Jed asked. "I don't follow. I don't think the people in Grants . . . at least not all of them are evil or that they should perish in the lava flows."
"Ok," Lucy said shaking her hand in Jed's face. "What is the plan? What are you and your ancient deadhead buddy going to do about all the people when you cause the earth to bleed this new and healthy skin? Forty feet of raging red hot lava running through the streets of Grants is not going to be a welcome visitor. If there are people in the way, they're gonna get baked. How are you gonna deal with that, hostene?"
Jed drew a deep breath and sat back in the drivers seat. He looked at Lucy then at the badlands rolling by. "I don't know," he finally admitted. "I don't know. But I'm sure Pajarito has an answer . . . I'm sure."
Lucy smiled and leaned against the open window. "I hope you're right hostene . . . I hope you're right."
The growing darkness enveloped the magnificent landscape of the Crownpoint Mesa country and everything in it, including Jed and Lucy in their aged pickup. Their headlights through the darkness were as lonely as two lost souls in the eternal emptyness of space.
They rolled on through the dark envelope until midnight found them on Santa Fe's familiar lanes, bouncing through the dirt road pot holes of Jed's neighborhood.
The final days of summer sped by for Jed and Lucy. They were together day and night. Whether they were lifting magaritas, cooking enchiladas, or finishing off a report at the computer terminal, they were close enough to touch.
They both knew too well that this level of closeness was drawing to an end. Lucy had classes beginning at Utah State the week of the tenth of September. As the dreaded day of her departure approached Lucy and Jed began to look at one another like abandoned puppies.
They had come in the short span of a few months from being only two randomly moving bodies to one life bound by love. Jed hoped he would have the strength and the will to continue his quest without Lucy beside him.
As Jed watched the bus pull away he felt lower than the oil stains on the pavement.
Jed's life had changed as never before over the past few months. Lucy had initiated most of those changes. She had gone through those changes with him and beside him and now suddenly she was not beside him. He felt empty and scared for the first time since this wild new turn in his life began. He was alone and walking in new and dangerous territory.

❖

CHAPTER VII · THE POOL OF TRUTH

Jed did not want to go home. He knew he would be able to feel her presence there and that would only make the pain worse. He headed for the plaza. He wasn't sure which watering hole he would put in at, but he was sure that drinking a pitcher of margaritas could not make matters any worse.

The Ore House balcony always had a special appeal to Jed on the warm and sunny days of late summer. He could see the balcony was crowded but he had set his mind on the location and nothing could change it.

Jed elbowed his way up the stairs past legions of touristas dressed in their finest newly bought Santa Fe fashions. He made his way to a corner of the balcony, parked his back against the stucco wall and ordered a pitcher of margaritas on ice. When his refreshment arrived he poured himself a tall glass and began to sip it as he gazed out across the plaza.

Jed was soon completely lost in his thoughts and quite oblivious to the drunken chatter all around him. He was looking across the plaza toward the mountains but he was seeing an inner vision that alternated between Lucy and all they had been through together and the devastated landscape that had caused all the suffering he wished to eliminate.

Jed was nearly through with his third glass of margarita mix when he was drawn from his inner visions to the other end of the Ore House balcony by the increasing volume of a familiar Pueblo song. He noticed the singing and accompanying drumming on the table was coming from a table full of what appeared to be Texas housewives dressed in cotton Mexican fiesta clothes. At the near end of the table with his back toward Jed a small man with the familiar Pueblo hair knot sticking out under a black cowboy hat was doing the singing and with exaggerated hand gestures was encouraging the covey of blond, buxom women to move to the ancient rhythm.

And move to the rhythm they did indeed. In increasingly loud and wild and obviously drunken movements the Texanas followed the lead of their Indian guide. They shook and they gyrated, some sitting in, and others standing on their chairs, until everyone on the balcony and for that matter on the street below was watching as though this was the height of entertainment on this afternoon.

One particular would-be native was dancing so vigorously that the string tie that held up her cotton sleeveless blouse was coming undone. She was oblivious to this development and her native guide either didn't notice or didn't care as he seemed to encourage her to move even more vigorously. Finally the string tie gave way to the rhythmic force of her undulating breasts and her top slumped to her waist. She stopped her gyrations for a moment but the crowd on the balcony and in the street below roared its approval and she proudly continued her exhibition. Not to be outdone by one of their own, the other Texanas one by one began to remove their tops and eventually there were no less than six blond drunken touristas dancing to the old indian's song on top of their chairs and their table on the Ore House balcony.

Apparently the commotion created by this exhibition attracted the attention of at least one of the dancer's husbands.

A strong Texas drawl was heard above the din of the crowd.

"Ruby! . . . Ruby! What in the hell are you doing up there?" The shout came from a tall man in an expensive Stetson hat and lizard boots who was standing on the sidewalk across the street from the Ore House with his hands on his hips and a look of complete disgust on his face. "You come down here right now and cover them titties up!"

The woman in question cast a drunken stare toward the man on the sidewalk then leaned over the balcony railing with her breasts hanging in the air.

"You can kiss my ass, Travis. I'm havin' fun for the first time since we left Lubbock. You are about a boring son of a bitch and I've found me a man who knows how to enjoy life."

She shook her platinum locks and rolled her eyes toward the diminutive pueblo man who stood politely and tipped his hat toward the Texan.

With the removal of his hat Jed realized for the first time that the old indian man was Pajarito. Jed was so amazed by this realization that he nearly fell off the balcony. After tipping his hat to the irrate husband Pajarito turned toward Jed and winked.

The Texan, by this point, was fuming obscenities and heading across the street toward the Ore House. "I'm gonna kill you! You fuckin' dirty indian!" were the last discernable words from the irate husband as he stepped onto the sidewalk below the balcony.

Jed was still looking at Pajarito with wild eyed wonder when the old indian gentleman bid his cordial farewell to the topless covey of Texanas and strolled calmly toward him.

"I think that man is very upset. What do you think Jed?"

Jed was speechless for a few seconds then with a chuckle he answered, "Yes . . . I think you're right."

"What should we do?" Pajarito asked with a gentle smile as he held his hat over his heart.

"Well," Jed began slowly in his best fake drawl. "I think we should probably move on . . . and soon."

Jed procured the heavy cotton rope used to close off sections of the Ore House restaurant and tied one end to the balcony railing as the sounds of a raging Texas bull grew closer. He lowered the other end to the sidewalk below and suggested with a gesture that Pajarito should exit forthwith by that means.

Jed followed Pajarito down the rope and the two of them casually strolled around the corner and down San Francisco Street. The sound of the commotion on the balcony quickly faded as they walked through parking lots and alleys toward the old federal building.

When they reached the shady park around the federal building Pajarito stretched out on top of a picnic table and pulled his hat over his face. Jed waited patiently and quietly for Pajarito to speak. When he did not after a long while Jed finally cleared his throat and spoke.

"Pajarito . . . Pajarito."

"Ugh." He grunted in response.

"Is there a reason we've met again? Is there something I need to do?"

Pajarito lifted his hat and squinted at Jed.

"Yes," he said softly. "There is always a reason . . . for everything. And there are many things you need to do . . . and learn . . . if you are to do this thing you say you want."

"Pajarito," Jed asked looking at the turquoise sky through the trees, "if I could cause the sacred mountain to erupt, how would the people who live around the mountain be saved from the lava?"

Pajarito smiled at the sky and began to hum the little pueblo song that he had performed with such wonderous effect at the Ore House. After a moment Pajarito pulled himself up on one elbow and looked at Jed.

"You know Jed," he began slowly, "that is a problem of this time and this space. I can help you find the right dance and the right knowledge to make this thing happen . . . but these are tools for use in another realm. I am of these other realms and exist here and now only because there is a need. You are that need right now. For problems and perils in this realm I depend on you to be the cacique. You will have to figure out a way to save the people if it's important to you. For me the healing power of the mountain is all that matters."

"But Pajarito," Jed began, "I don't see how . . . "

Pajarito held up his hand to silence Jed.

"Of course you don't see. That's why you asked me to help. You must learn to see that the answers you seek are all around you. Once in a while you get shown the light in the strangest of places if you look at it right. Ok?"

"Ok." Jed answered with some hesitation.

Pajarito sat up on the picnic table and put his ancient hand on Jed's shoulder.

"Remember, Jed, pay attention to as much of what's going on around you as possible. Try to be loose and not miss anything, even when you're standing in the check-out line at the grocery. And when you start to ski again soon, keep your eyes open for messengers. They will be around, it's just a matter of whether you can make them out in the bright light of day. Try moonlight if you're having trouble."

Jed looked puzzled but said nothing.

"Don't try to understand it young warrior. Just heed my advice. Things will come to you."

With that Pajarito smiled and began to walk away slowly. Jed watched the old man shuffle around the corner of the federal building and then he headed slowly back toward the plaza.

Jed made it to his truck and started driving home. As he neared Kaune's Market he remembered that his food supplies were greatly depleted and he pulled into the parking lot.

Inside he elbowed his way through the crowded store and found the essential beans, tortillas and chile. As he stood in the apparently stagnant check out line he looked around and tried to follow Pajarito's advice about paying attention. Nothing he looked at seemed particularly significant until his eye came to rest on the tabloid headlines in the rack by the checkout stand.

"I WAS BIG FOOT'S LOVE SLAVE! Missing Woman Returns Home With Fantastic Story!"

"Dead Woman Delivers Healthy Baby In Coffin!"

And then, there across the bottom of the front page of the Inquirer was a headline that did not make Jed chuckle.

"FRENCH TOWN EVACUATED AFTER NUCLEAR TERRORIST HOAX!"

Jed picked up the tabloid and quickly flipped through the pages until he found the full story. It seems that a nuclear terrorist group in France sent a warning letter on the letterhead of the French Nuclear Regulatory Agency to the country's parliament. A government spokesman was quoted as saying that there is enough unaccounted for plutonium on the planet that no such threat to set off a nuclear device could be ignored.

Jed was drawn back to reality by the grocery checker telling him that his bill was $4.60.

As Jed walked into the parking lot under the evening sky he knew he had basically found the way to get the towns around Mt. Taylor evacuated before the mountain erupted. He also knew that what Pajarito had told him was true. The answers are all around anyone who will see them.

Jed spent the bulk of the magnificent New Mexico fall working on a contract dig for The Museum of New Mexico. The Museum was conducting a dig on one of the pueblo sites around the village of Galisteo and Jed was their choice for managing the site and analyzing the finds.

Jed spent the entire month of October under a crystaline blue sky smelling the fresh earth in the sunshine and learning more about the ancient residents of this country.

He finished the last of his contract obligated reports for this and two other projects by late November and his eyes and his thoughts turned toward the newly snow covered mountains above town.

Jed had been a devotee of cross country skiing for many years. He considered it to be his principle yoga and the ideal system for maintaining health and sanity. There was something new driving him this year though as he began his solitary treks into the Pecos Wilderness. To be sure he was taking in much more of the sensory information all around him as Pajarito had advised and he had been practicing.

Something else was different about this season. He couldn't quite put his finger on it, but he felt it strongly. It was as though he was never truly alone no matter how far back into the wild country he went. It was an odd feeling, not particularly scary, but different. He often wondered if he would someday find Pajarito in the wilderness.

Something Pajarito had said at their last meeting kept coming back to Jed. He had said something about there being messengers in the mountains, something about their being hard to see in the light of day.

As the moon began its march toward fullness in January, Jed began to head out in the early evening for moonlit skiing. He had never tried skiing by moonlight before and at first he was a little frightened by the thought. He started on the wide safe trails of the Black Canyon campground. After an outing or two Jed found skiing by moonlight to be an exiting and invigorating experience. He also found that the way his senses responded to the subdued light was totally different.

On the night of the full moon in late January, Jed drove to the Big Tesuque campground and set out through the Aspens under remarkably bright illumination. Jed followed the Tesuque Creek trail until it intersected the Aspen Vista Road. He stopped to rest on the road and as he admired his surroundings he began to hear coyotes. They seemed to be all around him yipping and calling happily to one another. Jed smiled at the thought of these free roaming God dogs living out their lives here in this wild and beautiful place.

Jed decided it was time to ski on back through the aspens and after taking a warm up drink of brandy he checked his equipment and began the fast glide back down the trail. He was telemarking left and telemarking right through the deep powder snow. The chill air was biting at his face and whistling past his ears. He was in complete control and having a fine time.

Suddenly as he topped a small rise he found himself surrounded by running coyotes. To his amazement they seemed to be running on top of the deep snow, maybe even just above it. Jed continued to ski on down the trail with the canine escort all around him. They yipped and howled as they ran in a tight circle around Jed. Jed brought himself to a stop just before the trail crossed a tributary of Tesuque Creek. When he stopped the circling coyotes broke away from him and ran quickly down to an open section of the creek. They stood there circling this hole in the otherwise completely frozen stretch of stream and seemed to be looking very intently at the surface of the water.

Jed felt strongly compelled to go down on the ice bridge and see what the animals were looking at. He cautiously snow plowed down the steep embankment and inched his way out onto the snow covered ice bridging the stream.

When Jed reached the edge of the open pool, the coyotes were still looking at the water and they paid him no heed whatsoever. Jed looked into the water too and at first saw only the moon's reflection against the black water.

In a moment however the look of the water's surface began to change. The dark water and the moon's image began slowly to be replaced by an electric blue glow that gradually filled the pool. Jed did not experience any fear at this development, in fact the color of the pool seemed to bring on a feeling of immense well being.

Jed sensed a connection between himself and everything else that is or ever was. Somehow this pool reminded him of this knowledge which he felt he had always possessed but had lost access to.

This "Pool of Truth" stimulated a flowing sequence of technicolor images that opened many doors of understanding to Jed.

He "understood" in some considerable detail how he was connected to earlier generations of humanity and how he would now seek to find the dance that will connect the living power of the collective force of life.

Jed "saw" that he, or anyone who seriously wished to find the connections between what was and what is and what will be could do so, with diligence. Anyone could detect the ever present rhythm of this existence and move to it.

He "knew" with certainty that this after all was the nature of the dance. He understood the dance for the first time. What it can do. What it can effect here on our tiny planet. Jed also approached an understanding of how difficult it has become in this present day to affect anything beyond the physical realm. He came to see that a person living out his physical existence believing that there is nothing beyond the realm our heart beats in will have a very hard time finding the dance.

THE DANCE. That particular combination of rhythms that will open the doors between the realms and make available the collective energy of all life. The dance that will set up the proper frequency of life energy needed to cause an earth system to change.

At once Jed knew his potential and his limitations and a wave of fear caused him to shiver. With that tiny rush of fear the light faded and Jed was again standing on an ice bridge alone in the moonlight, looking at his reflection in dark water.

Jed looked around him at the stark white trunks of the aspens and the dark moonshadows they cast on the snow.

"The physical realm has its magic too," Jed thought as he began to climb back up the steep bank above the stream. He looked back at the pool from the trail, took a deep breath and another shot of brandy, and glided on back to his truck.

There was more skiing that winter both night and day. And there was more to experience and learn. The teachings of the Pool of Truth however remained a high water mark in Jed's quest for knowledge. Nothing surpassed the intensity of that lesson until well into the spring when the days of good skiing were numbered and the celebration of life and survival was everywhere.

Jed awoke at dawn on a fine clear April morning. He noticed there was scarcely any frost on the windows of his antique Willys. He had been taking notice for several days of the disappearing snow on the mountains above Santa Fe.

Jed knew that if a man was interested in any further skiing this season he had better get with it. He packed a lunch and water, threw his skis in the truck and headed up the mountain for the ski basin and the beginning of the Winsor Trail.

It was obvious in Santa Fe at 7,000' that spring had arrived. The apricot trees and a number of flowering shrubs were in full bloom. Jed quickened his pace a little as he turned onto the Hyde Park Road. He began to doubt that there would be enough snow to get into the headwaters of the Rio Nambe where he hoped to ski. This concern pushed him toward a higher rate of speed as though getting to the ski basin sooner would improve his chances of finding good snow.

When he arrived at the ski basin he was discouraged to see a number of stumps and rocks protruding from the snow field. He hastily grabbed his gear and started out for the Winsor trailhead. Halfway across the parking lot he realized he had left a sweater and his shell garment in the truck. He started back to retrieve these items, then looking at the nearly cloudless sky and feeling the relative warmth at nealy 10,000' he decided he wouldn't need them and proceeded on up the trail.

Jed carried his skis for the first mile through the crusted snow and ice to the Wilderness Gate. He was relieved to see a continuous, albeit crusted, cover of snow on the north facing slope above Rio Nambe. Jed quickly secured his bindings and glided off down the trail into the Nambe drainage.

The snow was still deep enough but the icy crust made control difficult and his velocity quickly became excessive. Many people would have turned around and gone home but Jed was not representative of the multitudes and he leaned and grunted his way through the turns.

At several points along the trail Jed skied over frozen moguls and became airborne for a few seconds. He handled these flights well though and proceeded on toward his objective.

As Jed approached the normally small stream that flows out of Nambe Lake he began to hear a tremendous roar. He was already moving through the woods on the icy trail at high speed. As he screamed through the last turn before the stream crossing he hit a sheet of solid ice and his velocity approached a terminal point beyond which control would surely be impossible.

This last stretch of trail before the stream was not so much steep as it was narrow. It left little room to turn and thereby slow his rate of advance and absolutely no hope of stopping. Jed felt that he was moving too rapidly to simply sit down where he was so he determined to ride the thing out.

"What the hell?" he thought. "I've made this turn at the rito many times."

Jed further assumed there would be an ice bridge to ski across or perhaps a small stretch of open water he could easily jump across.

He did not contemplate the scene that greeted him when he emerged from the forest into the open area just before the rito. The little stream that flowed down out of Nambe Lake was swollen out of its banks with meltwater and ragged chunks of ice.

Jed realized in an instant that his current course was rapidly delivering him to his death. He crouched into a deep telemark turn to his right. He managed with considerable effort to pull out of the frozen trail and up the steep, snow covered stream bank.

Unfortunately he was not able in the space available to reduce his speed in any meaningful sense. Before he could even think about what was happening Jed was launched off a four foot high snow ramp into the air space above the raging torrent.

For a few brief moments Jed was as graceful in flight as an eagle. The forces of gravity and poor aerodynamics soon diminished the quality of his flight noteably. Jed was certain he was about to ditch at sea. He tucked his body low onto the skis and prepared for what he expected would be a severe impact.

WHACK! . . . He hit pretty hard. But not that hard, and he wasn't wet or being carried to his demise by the flood. Jed opened his eyes and saw that he was face to face with a snowbank. He shook his head and pushed himself back from the bank. Jed managed a laugh when he saw that his skis were stuck in the snowbank about two inches above the water.

Jed pulled himself free and made his way back to the trail. He did a self assessment and determined that he was none the worse for the experience. Jed continued on the Winsor Trail until he reached the next stream crossing which was also swollen with melt water. He decided one crossing of a stream like that was enough for this day. Besides, he had to figure out how to get back across the first one.

Jed started working his way back through the woods covering the north slope of the ridge above the Rio Nambe. The snow was a lot better there and Jed thought he might intercept the stream from Nambe Lake at a higher point where the return crossing might be easier.

The skiing in the dark forest was good and Jed was having a fine time working his way back. As he skied through the woods Jed didn't really notice the gathering clouds or the sudden drop in temperature. It was the chill wind in his face when he stopped at the edge of a small clearing that finally made Jed take note of the weather changes. At first he was inclined to shrug it off as no big deal, but his instinct prevailed. There was something sinister about the darkening clouds. Jed shivered and decided it was time to get out.

Jed had mainly been skiing in circles among the big trees. Now he started back with serious intent. He had not faced the west wind for long before snow flakes began to sting his eyes. As Jed moved steadily into the storm the snowfall intensified. He cursed himself silently for not bringing the sweater and shell. His wool hat was in the pocket of the shell garment as were his gloves.

The spring snow squall turned quickly into a white out. Jed knew he was in serious trouble. By dead reckoning alone he moved on toward what he hoped was the stream. He knew the crossing could be deadly if an ice bridge were not found. He was certain he didn't have the strength to fight the current. Nonetheless he moved on in the direction he felt must be right. Jed felt that at least by getting to the stream he would know his instinct for direction was working.

Jed moved slowly through the trees. His visibility was very near to zero. Between his slow pace and lack of adequate clothing Jed had become quite cold. He struggled to keep his mind on the objective of reaching the stream. Jed recognized from experience the early symtoms of hypothermia. He was shivering and fighting a strong urge to lie down.

Jed was almost entirely out of strength and beginning to feel some genuine fear. He stopped and leaned against the trunk of an old Engleman Spruce. He looked up through the spiral of limbs and thought that this was a good place to die. He had very nearly accepted the inevitability of his death when the wind died a bit and he heard a strangely familiar sound.

It was the roar of a flood swollen stream. He stood up on his skis and shook himself off. He rubbed a cold hand across his face and trudged off toward the sound.

It seemed like an eternity before he reached the stream. When he could see the stream between wind gusts and snow squalls he knew for sure he couldn't cross, at least not at this point. With some considerable effort Jed started to move along the bank looking desperately for any hope of a safe crossing.

Jed was growing weaker by the minute. His vision seemed to be failing. Suddenly as he put his weight on his right ski something happened. The snow bank under him gave way and he tumbled in a heap onto an ice shelf above the torrent. Jed was stunned by the fall and too cold and weak to get up. Jed was certain that this was indeed the end.

Jed's fear of death passed rather quickly and was replaced with an odd dream like state in which he felt nothing. No fear. No cold. No pain.

He dreamed images of his recent past. The preparation for the quest that meant so much to Jed. Pajarito. His teachings. The magnificent beauty and magic he had felt. And Lucy . . . sweet Lucy. How he would love to hold her one last time. If only there were a way. Some help to get across the stream. "Where are the coyote brothers?" he wondered aloud. "Pajarito . . . Lucy?"

Jed was ready to release the veil of life when something jolted him back to the physical realm. It was extreme pain that diverted Jed from his death song. Something very heavy had been brought down hard on Jed's leg. His body jerked violently from the impact and he found himself sitting up and holding his thigh.

Suddenly he felt another jolt from behind. When he turned to see what had hit him he saw the hindquarters of a large animal disappear into the mist and snow above the stream. He heard a splash beside him and was amazed to see an elk starting to ford the stream and two more standing behind on the bank.

"ELK!" Jed said out loud. "ELK! WAPITI BROTHERS!"
Jed's numb mind was working as fast as it could under the circumstances. He knew somehow that this was his salvation. He just had to figure how to use this wonderful gift he had been given.

As he thought he watched several more elk make the crossing. The rate of snowfall had diminished a bit and Jed could see elk on both sides of the stream. He knew he was in the middle of a herd that had pushed a little too high a little too early looking for fresh grass.

The elk were crossing at a place they knew was shallow. The water was touching the bellies of the adults so Jed could see the depth. He decided he would sacrifice his skis and try to cross the stream on foot and walk out to the ski basin. He lowered himself off the ice shelf into the torrent and started to inch his way across.

Almost at once Jed was swept off his feet by the current. As he started to go under Jed reached out and grabbed the fur of a passing elk. To his amazement the elk simply walked on with Jed in tow. The elk dragged Jed onto the opposite bank and when it shook the water from its fur he was shaken loose too.

Jed lay motionless in the snow for a long while. The little spring snow squall passed and the golden light of sunset filled the forest. Jed slowly pulled himself to his feet and began to work blood back into his extremities. He exercised for a few minutes until the pain of being half frozen set in. With the return of feeling he began the walk back to the ski basin parking lot. The snow was hard packed and for most of the way Jed had no problem walking out on the frozen crust.

Jed stumbled out of the woods about an hour after dark. He was weak and cold but he managed to start his truck and get the heater cooking. It took another hour to thaw himself out sufficiently to drive on home. Jed ran a hot bath when he finally made it home and soaked in it until he truly believed he was alive again.

As Jed lay soaking he knew he had made it through a very important lesson. He promised himself he would never again be so blind as to assume he knew what nature would do.

Never again he promised . . . he hoped.

❖

CHAPTER VIII- AWAKE AT LAST

After his close encounter with death Jed's perception of the world changed. He felt vividly awake and energized. Nothing within his sensory range seemed trivial anymore. Even routine chores and short drives took on the character of grand adventures.

Jed quickly adapted to his new state of being and carried on with normal day to day activities as before. It even seemed to Jed that his contract bidding success had improved. He was awarded two small contracts in early May. One was a highway department survey and report, not unlike a dozen others he had done, and the other was his first contract with Los Alamos Labs.

The Los Alamos National Laboratory, (LANL) nuclear research facility had proposed to expand its laser technology testing range and that required a clearance under the cultural resource protection laws. Jed was given a sole source contract on a recommendation from the Museum of New Mexico.

Jed was almost overwhelmed by sensory input as he drove the familiar road up to Los Alamos. Cliff dwellings and petroglyph sites that he had studied in detail for many years seemed somehow different and worthy of close study. He ignored the urge though and drove on to his appointment with the LANL contract administrator.

Jed backed his truck into a space marked, CHIEF PROCUREMENT OFFICER, in front of a drab looking government office building. A steady stream of nuclear nerds flowed in and out of this and a dozen other equally drab labs and administrative offices.

As he walked down a long gray corridor past pictures of notable nuclear devices Jed realized just how deeply involved in causing the devastation around Mt. Taylor, LANL was.

By the time he reached the offices of contract services he had started to have some second thoughts about accepting this job.

As he sat waiting for Ms. Gloria Hackberry, LANL Contracts Administrator, he noticed something that changed his mind about the value of this contract. Jed noticed a stack of LANL letterhead stationary on the corner of Ms. Hackberry's secretary's desk. When the secretary walked down the hall to the ladies room, Jed slipped a few sheets of the letterhead into his leather bound notebook.

Jed scarcely heard Ms. Hackberry's chatter about the size, scope and importance of the new laser range as he sat silently and smiled. He knew this chance opportunity to work here gave him the ticket to pull off the nuclear terrorist threat that would clear the population from around Mt. Taylor before it erupted.

Jed completed the field survey work for the laser range in four days and had a final report prepared in another week. He was sure that the money he earned from these two contracts would see him through what he hoped would be a fruitful summer.

By the end of May the dominant force in Jed's life was his anticipation of Lucy's return. She had written Jed and explained that she planned to visit her grandparents for a few days after school was out, then would come to Santa Fe by June 8th.

Jed picked up Lucy on the appointed day and swept her quickly from the bus station to the mountains above town. They shared a picnic and each other on a worn soft Navajo blanket in the sun.

They talked and loved for the balance of the day and returned to Jed's house under the veil of summer's evening. Absence had not diminished their bond and reunion was a celebration of love and life.

When the physical imperative had lessened slightly Jed showed Lucy several versions of a nuclear blackmail letter on LANL letterhead. Each took a slightly different approach to informing the authorities that a "device" had been built with fissionable material stolen (along with the lab stationary) from Los Alamos.

Lucy laughed at first when she read the letters but turned serious after a few moments of thought.

"Jed . . . do you know what they will do to you if you get caught?"

"Sure," Jed answered also looking serious now. "They will take away my freedom. But they took away a little more than just your sister's freedom. And I don't intend to forget that. I would gladly trade my freedom for a chance to stop this deadly madness."

Lucy hugged Jed and told him she loved him.

"And," she continued, "I think the grandfathers must love you too."

They both agreed that any of the letters would probably produce the desired result given the level of paranoia regarding terrorism and the substantial amounts of missing fissionable material from Los Alamos and other nuclear facilities in the west.

After a few days of reunion celebration Jed suggested to Lucy that they should go try to find a cliff house ruin that a friend of Jed's had told him about. According to his colleague there was a substantial ruin in a large rock shelter at the head of a remote box canyon in the high mesa country between Dulce and Bloomfield. Jed had heard rumors of hidden and unmolested cliff ruins in this area for years but had not found the opportunity to explore the area adequately.

Lucy thought it sounded like a fine suggestion and she helped Jed sort out the camping gear for the trip. Jed packed his ropes and climbing gear in case the only way to approach the site was over the canyon rim rock.

On a fine, bright summer morning they slipped out of Santa Fe and headed north. After successfully negotiating Espanola their route took them along the cottonwood shrouded course of the Rio Chama. Only the dust and two dogs preparing to either fight or fornicate were to be seen stirring at the village of Abiquiu. They rolled on through the brilliant cliffs around Ghost Ranch and followed the road northward into the heart of Norteno country.

Cebolla was as dead as Abiquiu. Even the dogs were sleeping in the sun in front of the village store and cantina. Several hens scratching at the soil between skeleton automobiles were the sole signs of life as the little hamlet disappeared behind the travelers.

Jed and Lucy scarcely had to slow down as they passed through the Rio Arriba county seat at Tierra Amarilla. As they neared Chama however they caught up with the late twentieth century.

A line of rumbling and smoking RVs with Texas licence plates was backed up for more than a mile out of Chama. Jed sighed, then turned to Lucy and smiled.

"Things could be worse darlin. You could be on the New Jersey Turnpike with an ugly feller that didn't believe in personal hygiene."

"Ughhh." Lucy replied looking at the scenery and at Jed.

"I'm not complaining, at least I have nice things to look at here."

Jed nodded his head in agreement as he looked at Lucy and the magnificent Brazos cliffs in the distance beyond.

They crept along in the recreational traffic jam for twenty minutes or so before they were able to pull into a gas station and top off Jed's gas tanks.

Jed turned west out of Chama and was finally able to break out of the Texas second home column at the Broken Butt Saloon. Most of the RVs swung north at this point toward Pagosa Springs and the greater Colorado resort culture. Jed continued west toward the Jicarilla Apache agency town of Dulce and the wild high mesa country beyond.

Jed grabbed a couple of cans of beans at Joe Gonzales' grocery in Dulce just in case, and happily headed out of the last vestige of civilization he hoped to see for the next few days.

The Jicarilla country seemed to sparkle in the bright midday sun as Jed's old Willys rolled west. The smell of sagebrush filled the air out in the flats between rocky linear ridges and deer and antelope browsed unconcerned in the shadow of oil punps and storage tanks.

Jed crossed the Gubenador Arroyo and began to look for the next Forest Service road heading south. He spotted the combination oil well service and forest access road and turned left onto it. He stopped shortly after turning off the highway and without a necessary word between them both he and Lucy stepped out to turn in the front hubs.

Jed and Lucy proceeded generally southward on the dusty Forest Service road for over an hour before Jed spotted a three trunked Ponderosa Pine. His friend who knew about the site had said this tree was the signal to look for the next obscure two rut track to the right. Jed found the barely discernable track and with some considerable difficulty he made it through the deep bar ditch and continued toward his objective.

Progress was slow on this rough track and it was nearly an hour and a half later before the trail terminated on a large expanse of sloping slickrock above the head of a deep and narrow canyon.

Jed shut down his tired vehicle and he and Lucy stepped out on the bare slickrock and walked toward the canyon rim. About fifty feet from the rim they discovered a slit in the sandstone caprock. Water over the course of the millenia had carved this crevice along a joint fracture and through this window into the rock shelter below they saw a scene that put smiles on both their faces.

There against the back of the rock shelter looking as though it might still be in use was a small but magnificent cliff house ruin. Jed dropped to a prone position and twisted his head to get a better view through the crevice.

"God damn what a find!" he said with his face pushed as far as he safely could into the crevice. "It doesn't look like its ever been looted."

Jed stood up smiling and pushed back his hair.

"Let's find a way down there."

Lucy nodded agreement and the two of them spent the next half hour trying to find any possible route through the solid rimrock. After walking nearly a half mile along the west canyon rim, Jed shook his head and said, "I was afraid of this. That's why I brought the ropes. There won't be a break in this rimrock for a mile or more . . . let's go build an elevator."

Lucy rolled her eyes and looked a little pained. "Well I guess I have very little choice, hostene . . . but I don't really like this rope stuff . . . and I'm hungry."

Jed smiled and touched her on the shoulder. "You'll be fine. Its just like the way I taught you on the San Juan. Its easy, and we'll eat when we get to the ruin. Ok?"

Lucy looked at Jed for a second then answered with a tone of moderate skepticism. "O. . .K. I do trust you . . . so far."

When they returned to the head of the canyon Jed moved his truck as close as he could to the crevice and rigged his rappeling lines from the front bumper. He made a secure harness for Lucy from a length of one inch nylon webbing. He attached an "8 ring" descender to the double rappeling rope and connected it to Lucy's harness with a locking caribiner. Jed tied a belay line to Lucy's harness and handed her a set of gloves.

"All right darlin'," he said smiling. "Relax . . . walk over the edge . . . and kick off into a free fall at the bottom of the rimrock. And enjoy the ride. I'll join you in a few minutes."

Lucy was trembling a little but otherwise showed no outward sign of fear as she began to walk down the sheer ten foot thick wall of the rock crevice. Jed quietly encouraged her as she approached the bottom of the overhanging rock shelf. She flexed her legs a time or two before kicking off the rock and dropping into the free fall space of the rock shelter. She lowered herself slowly down the rope and landed gently on a dusty rock ledge about 120 feet below the rimrock.

When she shouted all clear Jed pulled up the rappeling gear on the belay line and tied a duffle bag full of all the required camping and feeding supplies on and lowered it to Lucy. He quickly followed down the double rappeling lines and in a few moments he was standing with Lucy between a two story room block and a kiva.

Although his first instinct was to begin exploring the ruin he ignored that imperative and began instead to cook up a pot of beans heavily laced with green chile and onions. In only a few minutes he and Lucy were happily soaking tortillas in the spicy mixture.

After hunger was adequately driven away, for the moment, Lucy and Jed set out to systematically explore the almost pristine ruin. It was so dry and protected in the deep rock shelter that even some remnants of anazasi basketry and cotton fabrics remained here and there next to whole pots and bowls. Jed touched nothing as he moved carefully through the room blocks. He kept careful notes and tried to sketch everything he saw.

In a small chamber carved into the solid sandstone of the rock shelter Jed found a pile of assorted human bones. He knew this was not a burial from the haphazard condition of the bones. And on closer inspection he found evidence that the bones had been rather purposefully cut with stone implements and some of them showed clear evidence of having been chewed by human teeth.

"What is this?" Lucy asked looking a bit confused.

"This," Jed answered slowly. "Is evidence of just how hard times got before these folks abandoned this site. I've seen it before in digs and at other ruins. It appears that due to warfare, or famine, or both or, something else, folks around here about eight or nine hundred years ago took to eating one another and from there on in the record we don't see Anazasi anymore."

Lucy looked thoughtful for a moment then said, "Maybe it was my ancesters coming into this country that caused their downfall."

Jed looked at her and answered, "That's about as good a theory as any. Maybe we should ask Pajarito when we see him again."

Jed and Lucy continued their exploration of the ruin until the weakening light of dusk convinced them that they should set up their camp for the night. They laid a canvas tarp on the flatest bit of ground they could locate and spread their blankets and other gear on it. The fading sunset colored the kiva next to their tarp as Jed gathered firewood for the night.

Lucy and Jed faded into the sweet sleep of love's embrace as the last glowing coals from their fire cast a dim orange light on the shelter. Jed slipped into a familiar dream state where it was unclear if he was the dreamer dreaming the dream or if the dream created the dreamer.

In Jed's dream he was walking somewhere in a heavy mist. He walked on without purpose until the mist began to fade. He realized in his dream state that he was walking in the canyon just below the cliff house ruin where he and Lucy were camped. As he looked up at the rock shelter he could see a number of people at work and play in the pueblo.

No one seemed to notice Jed as he walked into the space between the room block and the kiva. A number of routine activities were taking place all around him. Several potters were working on ceramic vessels. Some were connecting coils of clay into the desired shapes. Others were applying the familiar black on white glazes with yucca leaf brushes. In several locations women were grinding corn and other seeds on stone metates.

As Jed the dreamer stood watching the scene around him his attention was diverted by the sound of a staccato drum beat. He turned toward the sound and saw a line of masked dancers emerge from the back of the rock shelter. No one seemed to notice these Kachinas except Jed. The daily routine continued all around him without any sign of acknowledgement of the sacred procession.

Each Kachina had either a drum or a gourd rattle or a juniper rasp. They seemed to each be creating sound without regard for the others, but collectively they created a rhythm that seemed both familiar and exotic.

As the Kachinas brushed by Jed he knew without a word of instruction that he was to follow. The masked messengers of the creator climbed the stone and adobe steps of the kiva and one by one after first making three false starts each descended the ladder into the ceremonial chamber.

Jed did likewise and soon found himself seated along with the Kachinas on a low bench that circled the interior of the kiva. The kiva was dimly lit by a small fire on a raised platform opposite the sipapu. There were four even smaller fires in niches along the circular kiva wall that Jed knew represented the four cardinal directions.

After a few moments of silence a column of white smoke began to rise from the sipapu. From out of a hidden niche or somewhere, another figure appeared. Jed knew in an instant this was a cacique and in another instant he saw that this cacique was none other than Pajarito.

Jed the dreamer smiled as the Kachina percussion symphony started up again. Pajarito moved fluidly around the interior of the kiva and touched each Kachina on the chest as he passed them. Pajarito paused in front of Jed and did the same to him. Jed began to feel incredible warmth where Pajarito had touched him. For some reason he tried to stand but could not. His legs collapsed and he fell to the floor of the kiva with his face above the sipapu.

As Jed looked through the window between the worlds he saw the entire earth floating in space. The mother planet looked like a blue jewel in a sea of black velvet. As he watched Jed began to see irregular white lines of what appeared to be electricity crackling over the surface of the earth.

Occasionally one or more of the lines of energy would seem to arc to various points on the earth and a bright flash of light would occur. Jed gradually became aware of a definite syncronization between certain rhythmic components of the Kachina's music and the bright flashes of light. Jed began to understand that the dance and the music and the rhythm of the Kachinas was a part of the earth and that all the vital earth processes were controllable.

Jed came to see very clearly as he peered into the infinite that he was also a part of the dance of life. He saw that the only difference between himself and anything else was molecular arrangement. He was reminded again that he had the potential to succeed in his quest.

Jed raised his head from the sipapu to look at Pajarito and instead saw nothing except darkness in the kiva. He looked up at the kiva entry and saw the dim light of an approaching dawn. Suddenly he realized he was no longer the dream but instead he was again the dreamer. Now however the dreamer was awake and stuck in the kiva with no ladder.

Jed slumped back against the kiva wall and tried to think of a way to get out but no solution came to him. Finally in desperation he began to call out to Lucy.

"Lucy . . . Lucy wake up and help me!"

Lucy emerged from a sound sleep and slowly sat upright. She looked beside her and saw that Jed was gone.

"Jed?" she called his name weakly at first then louder. "Jed! Where are you?"

"I'm here," he answered. "In the kiva."

Lucy stood up and wrapped a blanket around her bare shoulders then walked cautiously toward the kiva. She stood over the entry squinting into the darkness within.

"Is that you Jed?"

"Yes. And I can't get out. There's no ladder."

"What are you doing in there?" she asked shaking her head. "How did you get down there without a ladder?"

"I'm not sure," Jed answered. "I guess you could say I was sleep walking."

"Well," Lucy said yawning. "Nothing surprises me anymore. I don't know how to get you out so I'm gonna go back to sleep."

As Lucy shuffled away from the kiva entry Jed shouted. "Wait! Wait a minute Lucy. Just tie a rope to a big rock and lower it down. I'll climb out."

Lucy did not respond and after a few minutes Jed began to worry that she really had gone back to sleep.

"Lucy . . . Lucy are you there?"

His answer came in a few minutes when she lowered one end of a braided climbing rope down to him. He pulled himself out of the ten foot deep chamber with only a little difficulty at the entry and smiled at Lucy when he emerged.

"Sorry to bother you so early in the morning darlin' . . . but you're my only friend in the neighborhood."

Lucy only grunted and continued to tend her fire and flip the pancakes she had hastily concocted on the rusty Coleman grill.

"I really am sorry Lucy. Its hard to explain what happened. I thought I was dreaming of being in the kiva . . . but maybe I'm dreaming of this . . . I really don't know."

"That's all right hostene. I can tell you from my dreams that this place is full of chindees. They were pinching my butt and pulling my toes all night. I wouldn't be at all surprised if they put you in the kiva for fun. These Anasazi ghosts can be real mean little bastards. I know — I grew up among them."

Jed brushed back his disheveled hair. "Lucy, I really don't think there's any malevolence here . . . maybe some mischevy . . . but no ill will. Pajarito was in my dream . . . if it was a dream . . . and he means us no harm, I'm sure."

"Sure . . . sure Jed. Do you think that old pueblo ghost fart is gonna care if you get vaporized by dabbling in Anasazi magic? Noooooo . . . he'll just keep on tripping along in whatever space it is he exists in. My granny told me that Anazasi is bad medicine and she never lies. Now I have spoken. Get over here and eat some pancakes."

After breakfast Jed and Lucy resumed their detailed exploration and documentation of the ruin. In all, Jed measured and sketched over fifty perfect or nearly perfect pieces of classic Chacoan pottery. He also documented eleven remnants of various styles of basketry. Jed knew this was a very important site and he decided to say nothing about it to anyone, at least for a while.

By mid-afternoon Jed had cataloged the artifacts in all but one of nineteen rooms in the little cliff house complex. He was carefully drawing a fragment of woven yucca fiber when Lucy shined her flashlight into a small depression against the back wall of the tiny room.

"What is that?" Lucy asked as she trained her light on what appeared to be a large pot sherd with a clean round hole through it.

Jed turned from where he stood crouched over the basket fragment and took a few cautious steps toward where Lucy's light beam was pointing.

He shined his own light on the fragment and carefully brushed away a little of the soil and dust from its edges.

"I think this is an entire bowl, not just a sherd."

"Why does it have that little round hole in it Jed? It looks like somebody ruined that bowl on purpose."

"You're right!" Jed answered smiling. "You see that a lot in Anasazi and Mimbres sites. They would punch a hole through a dead person's favorite bowls and include them in . . . burials. Oh shit . . . this is probably a burial."

Jed stood up as far as the low roof would allow and carefully shown his light around the funeral bowl looking for any other evidence of a burial. There were some more pottery sherds, a few shell and torquoise beads, some obsidian arrow points, and to Jed's horror under his left boot a human scull turned on its side. The scull was brown with age and mineral staining and the jaw, complete with a full set of teeth, was frozen agape in the soil matrix giving the impression of a perpetual scream.

"Jesus Christ!" Jed groaned. "Let's back on out of here. I should've been paying more attention. I try to always show respect for burials . . . but I think standing on this guys head more or less violates that principle."

Lucy shook her head in disbelief. "My granny said this was about the worst thing you can do to Anasazi. Yes, Jed let's back on out of here . . . and then lets get on out of the rock shelter before dark. I am not spending the night in this place again. Not now . . . not after this!"

Jed nodded agreement and the two of them began to walk as quickly as conditions would allow. As they moved along they became conscious of a low, but steadily increasing moaning sound. Lucy touched Jed on the shoulder and asked in a low tone, "What is that?"

Jed turned his head to the left then to the right, rubbed his chin and answered, "Its the wind. Just a canyon wind whistling through the room blocks. That's all."

"Wind?"

"Wind!"

The volumn of the sound increased to almost deafening proportions by the time they emerged from the room blocks. The wind was indeed blowing incredibly hard straight into the rock shelter. It seemed that all the loose dust and sand for miles around had made its way to this particular rock shelter and was being circulated at high velocity by the strangest windstorm either Jed or Lucy had ever seen.

Verbal communication was impossible but with signals both Lucy and Jed indicated they agreed it was time to get out. Jed had the simple camp packed and ready to go in less than five minutes. Lucy in the meanwhile was putting on her climbing harness and reminding herself of how the jumar ascenders worked. Jed checked her climbing gear and signalled her to begin climbing out. He held the bottom of her rope to ease the first few feet of jumar work and he watched as she all but disappeared into the dust tempest.

It seemed to Jed an awfully long time before he saw the climbing rope pulled up suddenly five or six feet and then dropped again in a few seconds. To Jed this was proof Lucy had made it to the top and had pulled up a few feet of slack to ease removal of the jumars and climbing harness. In a moment the climbing gear came sliding down the rope for Jed to use and this confirmed her safe arrival.

Jed tied the camp gear to the bottom of his climbing rope, rigged his harness, secured his jumars, and began the 120' free climb to the overhanging rim rock. As Jed climbed the velocity of the wind increased and the strange howling sound became almost unbearable.

Jed looked up the rope to see if he could see the rimrock through the dust. He could not at that point, but he could see that the airborne grit was taking its toll on the rope. Threads were frayed all along the rope and in one place, ten or fifteen feet above him the outer sheath on the braided nylon was completely worn through.

Jed realized quickly that he was on a very tenuous lifeline. He quickened the pace of his climb as much as circumstances and his personal energy would allow. Within a minute he inched past the dangerously frayed spot and from that vantage he could see the rimrock only ten feet above him.

As he crept up the last few feet of rock Jed was amazed to see Lucy standing and smiling under a clear late afternoon sky.

"Isn't this wierd?" she asked still smiling as he emerged from the localized tempest. "There's not a breath of wind up here and no sign of a dust storm in the canyon. Its only there down in the rock shelter. It's the chindees for sure."

Jed pulled himself onto the slickrock and unharnessed. He pulled up his climbing rope first with the camp gear in tow. He walked over to his truck and tossed the duffle bag in the back. As he started back toward the crevice his foot somehow became entagled with the belay rope and he felt a hard jerk on the line. He fell on the slickrock and rolled to within a few inches of the crevice.

Sweat dripped from his brow as he pushed himself up from the rock. As he looked through the crevice he saw that the dust phenomenon had ceased. The cliff house ruin looked as pristine and inviting as the first time he saw it the day before.

Jed sat silently on the edge of the crevice and looked at the ruin as he coiled his ropes. The sun was close to touching the western horizon when Jed finally threw the last rope in his truck and walked over to where Lucy was standing.

"You know Lucy," he said softly into her ear as he hugged her. "I think you're right. There are too many chindees around here. Let's go home."

Lucy was asleep before they reached the pavement and remained that way until they reached Santa Fe shortly before midnight. All through the silent darkness Jed drove and thought about the path he was on. There was no turning back now. He was in touch with facets of the world he either forgot or didn't know existed. It was exciting and scary and enlightening and frightening and it was real, and he was never looking back.

CHAPTER VIII - FINAL EXAMS

Mid June in northern New Mexico is exquisite. Daytime temperatures are near perfect. The monsoon usually has not arrived. The skies are clear and the sun is bright. Love or any powerful passion can easily dominate feeling in such a season.

No waking moment of love was wasted by Jed or Lucy whether it be in the mountains or the desert or lying in a stream. After a day of such activities in the sun and water of White Rock Canyon, Jed, who arrived at the canyon rim first, was surprised to find Pajarito sitting on the hood of his truck.

"Pajarito!" was about all Jed could muster for words before Lucy walked through the rimrock panting, still naked except for her sandals from her day on the river. She looked up as she finished the last little grade before Jed's truck and saw he and Pajarito smiling.

"Jesus Christ, Jed! Why didn't you tell me this old pervert was up here? Where the hell did you come from anyway?"

Lucy was obviously quite angry as she pulled on her cutoffs and a t-shirt.

"Lucy I'm sorry," Jed tried to explain. "I didn't know he was up here either . . . and I don't think words can really describe where he comes from . . . and he's not a pervert . . . I'm sure he didn't do this so he could see your body."

Pajarito raised his hand to his mouth to cover a little smile.

"Thank you my son. Your defense of me is touching . . . and most of it is true . . . I must tell you though that I am something of a pervert by the standards of this day . . . and I did show up now and here to see your lady in all of her loveliness . . . I am deeply sorry if it offends you."

Pajarito stood on the wide fender of Jed's Willys and bowed deeply toward Lucy. She folded her arms across her chest and breathed deeply blowing out hard through her nostrils. She looked like a mustang filly ready to kick.

In another moment though she smiled and returned the bow saying, "I accept your apology . . . you old pueblo pervert."

The three of them climbed into Jed's old truck and headed out across the wide expanse of the Caja Del Rio toward Santa Fe.

After a few minutes of silent bouncing across the rocks and ruts of the Caja, Pajarito turned his face from the hills to Jed and asked, "How strong do you feel young warrior?"

"Strong," Jed answered. "Very strong!"

"How wise do you feel?"

"Wise enough!"

"Do you know the dance?"

"I know what the dance is all about, and I know when the time comes I will know the dance."

Jed smiled and nodded his head to emphasize the statement.

Pajarito also smiled and began to drum a little rhythm with his fingers on the outside of the truck door. After a prolonged silence Pajarito stopped druming and turned again to Jed.

"Fine! Very good then. Its time to test your knowledge . . . and your power . . . and your courage."

Jed could scarcely contain himself.

"All right. Finally, we're gonna go to Mt. Taylor and do it. Dance that fuckin' mountain into an eruption."

Pajarito tried to say something but Jed continued, "We're gonna do it on the solstice right? June 21st or so right?"

Pajarito held up a weathered hand to silence Jed.

"You're right about the solstice, that would be a good time to allign earth forces . . . and maybe we will go to dance then on Mt. Taylor . . . but before you take on that task we need to have a test . . . a final examination of your will."

Lucy and Jed both turned their heads toward the old cacique as he continued.

"If you wish to continue on this quest to affect the destiny of the earth you need to practice your craft. If we are of a like mind on this thing when I finish speaking we will prepare to go to Sierra Ladrone tomorrow. There you will dance young warrior . . . and if your will and your courage are strong enough, the earth will move."

The three riders bounced along silently for several minutes before Lucy finally spoke.

"Pajarito. . . my man has been your student in this quest for nearly a year. He has trusted that your motivation is like his, to heal a large piece of the mother earth. I trust him and love him and his quest is mine. Of course we are still with you. This is the only hope of making the land healthy again. But let me tell you one thing you old cacique or chindee or whatever you are. My man had better come back from this dance alive or I will search you out in whatever realm you hide in and teach you the meaning of hell!"

Pajarito contorted his face, then smiled.

"Jed . . . you have something here in this fine woman that is more powerful than any other force of nature . . . she loves you and will fight for you against any odds. Certainly there is a risk to your physical being from what you are about to do. I cannot lessen that . . . but you can by your thoughts and your actions. You or anyone who practices, can be the instrument of constructive change on this planet, and walk away from a moment of connection with the infinite intact . . . if you are ready."

Somehow Pajarito's words caused a great feeling of well being to settle over the old truck and its occupants as they rolled along the dusty tracks of the Caja. That night the three of them laughed and ate and drank and prepared gear for the final exam at Sierra Ladrone. Sometime after midnight Lucy noticed that Pajarito had silently departed their company. As she and Jed lay together later, under cotton sheets, quietly breathing, Lucy said in a whisper, "Pajarito will be back in the morning when its time to go."

"I'm sure you're right darlin." Jed answered slowly.

They drifted off to sleep in a tangled embrace, dreaming, and glowing with that most powerful of forces . . . love.

As predicted, Pajarito was sitting on the tailgate of Jed's truck when he carried his camping gear out the next morning.

"Good morning Jed. Its a fine day to climb a mountain in the desert. The lines of energy under the earth are converging to the south. Are you ready to ride them?"

Jed smiled as he threw his gear in the truck.

"I'm as ready as I will be in this life."

Jed and Lucy and Pajarito were rolling south before mid morning under a brilliant cloudless sky. They slid through the smog and traffic of Albuquerque and into the beginnings of the mesquite and creosote country. Pajarito instructed Jed to drive to Socorro then west to Magdelena before turning north on the dusty BLM track to Riley and the Rio Salado.

Jed topped off his gas tank in the painfully dull little town of Socorro before pulling out of the Rio Grande Valley and heading into the lovely high plains on the flanks of Sierra Magdalena. At the old west cattle rail head of Magdelena they left the pavement and raised a twenty mile plume of dust before crossing the damp sands of Rio Salado.

A few miles south of the river and the almost ghost town of Riley, Pajarito asked Jed to stop. Without a word of explanation he walked around the front of the truck and off to the west for a few yards then vanished.

Lucy and Jed looked at each other then back to the spot where they last saw Pajarito. In a few moments they both got out of the truck and walked over to where he vanished. To their surprise they saw a cave entry under a limestone ledge. Jed trotted back to his truck and pulled an old carbide miners lamp from his gear. He started the flow of water over the calcium carbide and in less than a minute he had a bright acetelene flame burning in front of the lamp reflecter. He started cautiously into the cave entry then looked back to see if Lucy was following. She was not. She was still standing out in the bright light and when Jed looked at her she folded her arms and shook her head.

"No Jed . . . I think I'll stay out here and watch the truck."

Jed smiled and nodded agreement before disappearing into the cavern. The cave passage dropped off suddenly and curved sharply to the left. At the bottom of a fifty foot slope the passage flattened out and the roof became noticably higher. Jed played his light around the large room until he noticed that a number of bats were fluttering down from the cave roof. When Jed shown his light straight up he saw the entire roof of this large room was covered with roosting bats. There were hundreds, if not thousands, of Mexican Free Tail Bats roosting and fluttering around the room.

As Jed watched the living spectacle he was startled by a touch on his arm. He turned quickly and in the reflected light from the cave roof he saw Pajarito.

"Come my son. We've disturbed our brothers here enough. I have what I came for." He held up a small leather pouch. "Come now," he said again. "Let us go back to the land of the light."

Back at the cave entry Pajarito sat down on a sandy spot and motioned for Jed to do the same.

"Here young warrior," he said holding up the small leather pouch, "is a special type of mineral paint that is only found here in this cave. If you mix it with the juice of a prickly pear in full bloom and apply this paint to your body you will be protected from most harm."

Jed took the pouch full of white powder from Pajarito as they both stood up. They walked back to the truck where Lucy was sitting on the hood. Pajarito scratched his chin and rocked on his heels in the deep dust of the BLM road. He looked off toward the summit of Sierra Ladrone in the distance.

"Now," he said still looking at the mountain. "We need to go on down the road a little further and hide this truck and set up a camp."

Pajarito instructed Jed to drive up the next big drainage as far as he could, and hide the truck somehow. In a few minutes Jed was idling at the bottom of a big arroyo and everyone in the truck was looking at a five strand barb wire fence and a large yellow sign.

U.S. BUREAU OF LAND MANAGEMENT
WILDERNESS STUDY AREA
CLOSED TO VEHICULAR ENTRY
Except Valid Existing Mineral Claim Holders

Jed looked at Pajarito and pointed at the sign. "Doesn't look like we're gonna drive up that drainage."

Pajarito looked hard at the fence, then raised his eyebrows. "No Jed look, they made a gate for us."

And indeed there was a wire ranch gate just to the left of the sign.

"Pajarito, that gate's for the mineral claimants. They're the only ones that won't get in trouble for driving in there."

Pajarito frowned and looked at Jed. "Nonsense!" he grunted waiving his hand out the window. "No one owns the earth. We all have the right to go anywhere we want as long as we harm nothing and no one. Go on over there . . .I'll open the gate."

Jed looked at Lucy, she nodded agreement, and he smiled and drove on over to the gate.

Pajarito held the wire gate open as Jed drove through and he trotted on back to the waiting truck after closing it. He pointed upstream with his chin and Jed drove on up the wide sandy arroyo. Soon they were well away from the fence and the Riley-Bernardo road and out of sight.

The arroyo bottom began to narrow after a couple of miles and large rocks became more numerous and difficult to avoid. Pajarito pointed ahead at small cluster of cottonwoods.

"Hide your truck in those trees. This is the best place . . . there's a spring over there in the rocks too."

Jed complied without a word and soon all three were standing in the fine shade of tall cottonwoods listening to the birds and bugs.

With his hand lightly on Lucy's shoulder Pajarito smiled at her.

"Lucy Begay," he said softly. "I know you have not always trusted me or liked me being around your man. And maybe still you will not listen to me . . . but I will ask you to stay here with the truck . . . and be prepared to leave in a hurry if something strange begins to happen. This I ask for your sake as well as Jed's. He must make the right moves and sing the right melodies on his own. . . or the earth will not move. And if he doesn't pay attention, the earth might react more violently than we want . . . right now."

Jed looked at Lucy and said, "He's right babe. This is some heavy medicine we're talkin' about here. I'm proud that you've stuck with me through all of this. Most women would have left and had me committed. Please stay here with the truck. I'll come back . . . I promise."

Lucy looked at the peaks of Sierra Ladrone, then at the sky, then at Jed. "All right Jed. I'll stay here this time. But no promises for the future!" She pointed her finger and stomped her boot to emphasize the statement. Pajarito turned to Jed and spoke. "Now young warrior, we have preparations to attend to."

Lucy watched silently as Jed and Pajarito walked into the hills above the spring. She set about creating a comfortable camp for the night in the truck bed and boiling up some spring water for tea.

The sun was approaching the western horizon when Pajarito and Jed walked in with a sack full of cactus and other plants. Without a word Pajarito began to prepare a pasty mixture of various plants and flowers. When the mixture was well blended Pajarito called for Jed to bring him the pouch of white mineral paint. He mixed about equal portions of paint and plant puree and turned to Jed with a smile.

"All right now, take off all your clothes."

Jed hesitated for a moment.

"Go ahead," Pajarito laughed. "Everyone here has seen your hiney before. Come on I have to paint you before the sun goes down."

Jed was blushing and Lucy could barely contain her laughter as he began to undress. When he finished Pajarito motioned for Jed to come over and he quickly tied his sash into a breech cloth on him. Pajarito then began to paint designs on Jed's face and body.

As the sun slid beneath the western horizon Pajarito finished the last of Jeds body paint. He stood back and admired his handiwork for a few seconds then said, "Now . . . it is time to climb to the summit. We should be there before the moon is fully overhead."

Jed looked at Lucy who smiled weakly and raised her hand and wiggled her fingers in a goodbye gesture. He returned the greeting and turned back toward Pajarito who immediately began to walk rapidly up the arroyo. Jed followed with more than a little trepidation and looked back one more time at Lucy before he and his cacique guide rounded a bend in the drainage and disappeared.

There were no words between Pajarito and Jed as they climbed incessantly for the next two and a half hours. Eventually the drainage terminated at the base of a steep granite outcrop. By then the three quarter moon was nearly directly overhead and Pajarito finally broke the silence.

"You must go on alone from here. For this test I cannot help you beyond what has already been done. Climb straight up this crevice and you will reach the summit. Once there it is up to you to make contact with the infinite. Think of all you have learned . . . pray . . . and find the dance. Now you are the cacique . . . practice your craft. I will be here when you return."

With that Pajarito made himself comfortable on the rocks, closed his eyes and fell straight away to sleep. Jed looked around at the magnificent scene before him, thought of his task, felt a tiny shiver of fear, then started toward the summit.

It was still a considerable climb up the steep and rugged granite to the summit of Sierra Ladrone. When Jed finally pulled himself onto the highest point he was winded and tired. The brilliant three quarter moon was directly overhead. Jed lay on the ragged summit looking at the moon until his breathing returned to normal. He pulled himself to his feet and began to move slowly looking for some indication that would cue him to the nature of the dance.

Jed tried singing little pueblo songs he had learned over the years. He tried praying and moving his feet to the rhythm of his heartbeat. He tried everything he could think of but nothing seemed to be working. Finally in exhaustion and desparation he lay back down on the irregular surface of the mountaintop.

In only a very few moments and without really meaning to Jed slipped into the deep sleep of the weary. He began to dream. In his dream he saw himself lying on the mountain. Off on the distant horizon in each of the cardinal directions he saw a bright point of light, like four equal and opposite morning stars.

From behind each bright star he watched a colorful rattlesnake emerge. A white snake with black speckles from the north, blue from the east, red from the south and yellow from the west. As each of the snakes crawled toward him it left a shimmering trail of pulsating particles. The snakes crawled directly to Jed the dreamer on the mountaintop. When they reached him they coiled their bodies around his and they and Jed and the whole mountaintop began to glow with a brilliant irridecsent blue.

Jed stood up on the summit in the dream, and the snakes began to crawl around his feet in a clockwise motion. He took a slow step off of the mountaintop and onto the shimmering particle path the white snake of the north had left. He took four slow and measured steps toward the northern horizon, then turned and with similar steps returned to the summit. Jed, the dream dancer, repeated this process along the colorful snake paths in each of the other cardinal directions and then found himself standing on the summit with a cottonwood staff in his right hand.

He held the staff high above his head and a brilliant beam of white light from deep in space made contact with it. Immediately, Jed thrust the staff through the summit and deep into the heart of Sierra Ladrone. The center of the earth seemed to let loose a moan and the four rattlesnakes slithered along their particle trails back to the horizon.

Jed found himself suddenly awake and alone on the summit feeling the mountain tremble beneath his feet. When the last of the aftershocks faded Jed cut loose with a howl like a wounded coyote. He knew he had found the dance. As a dreamer to be sure . . . but the dance nonetheless.

Jed crawled back down the granite crevice to where he had left Pajarito. The old cacique was lying on his stomach watching two lizards mate in the growing light of dawn. He did not look up from the lizards as Jed stood breathless above him.

"That was a pretty good tremor young warrior. You danced well . . . once you were the dreamer. You may not have that luxury when we go to the sacred mountain. You will need to prepare yourself in advance."

Jed's elation faded a bit as he listened to Pajaritos words.

Pajarito turned to Jed and smiled. "Don't despair young warrior, you have done well. You were chosen for this quest because you are uniquely qualified to succeed. You have proven that trust was well placed. I warn you about the sacred mountain only for your own protection. What you must do there is far more difficult than this test. You may fail. You may die . . . but you may also heal the earth where it has been so badly wounded. We will all know which way that wind will blow very soon. Very soon indeed."

Jed followed Pajarito back down the mountain to the camp in the cottonwoods where Lucy waited. Lucy ran to Jed when she saw him round the last bend before the cottonwood spring.

"God I'm glad to see you Jed!" She cried as she hugged him.

"What a light show!" she said standing back to look at Jed. "I watched the whole thing last night. It was wild and beautiful. It scared me a little when the ground began to shake. Are you ok?"

"I'm fine," Jed answered. "Just fine."

After coffee and hotcakes and a detailed explanation of all that happened the previous night, camp was broken and the three began the journey back to Santa Fe.

Jed took the north route out and thereby completed a large circle of Sierra Ladrone. When he reached Interstate-25 he turned his old truck radio on to a country music station out of Socorro. When the news on the hour came on the lead story was the 4.2 quake that had occurred shortly before dawn with its epicenter near Lemitar. Everyone in the old Willys was smiling when the cheatin' songs continued.

The familiar landscape of the Rio Grande valley and the hypnotic rumble of the engine soon led to sleep for Lucy. Jed was also a little tired as he emerged from the vehicular morass of Albuquerque. He was brought back to full wakefulness though by the sight of Mt. Taylor on the western horizon. He knew the real test of his will would come there on that distant highland, and very soon.

CHAPTER IX- GRADUATION

Pajarito helped Jed and Lucy unload the truck when they arrived in Santa Fe, then explained that he had important matters to attend to. Before he departed he gave Jed some very specific instructions.

"You must send your warning letters to the State Police by no later than day after tomorrow. They will need a little time to react and plan the evacuation of the towns around Mt. Taylor. Also, you must begin a fast on that same day. Eat nothing at all and drink only water with a little red chile powder in it. Prepare to set up a base camp and be ready to leave on a moment's notice. I'll be back when its time to go. Oh yes, and try to refrain from fornication for a few days."

With that advice he dissappeared through the garden gate and into the twilight.

Lucy looked Jed up and down then wrinkled her mouth. "Ok . . . you're not gonna eat . . . and we can't make love. All right, if that's the deal then so be it . . . but I can tell you right now that I'm gonna eat enough for both of us!"

She walked into the kitchen and began to rattle around the pots and pans and soon the smell of sauteed onions and garlic was wafting throughout the house.

"Wait a minute," Jed called out from the living room. "I don't have to start this fast until day after tomorrow . . . and he was not specific in the prohibition on sex!"

The sound of Lucy's laughter from the kitchen made Jed smile. He carefully tip toed behind her and reached under her cotton tank top and gently siezed a breast.

She yelped but quickly began to purr as she pushed her hips back into Jed's mid section. They both dropped to the Saltillo floor and violated Pajarito's advice as though it were either the first time in a long while or the last time forever.

The next day Jed prepared a final copy of the nuclear terrorist ransom letter. He smiled as he read it.

"TO THE CORRUPT AND OMNIPOTENT PURVEYORS OF EVIL"

"You and all of you who have unleashed the great demon of nuclear power on this planet hear this warning.

From among you we have come. We know your secrets and your power is ours. While helping you to corrupt the creative force we were awakened to this evil and have vowed to stop you.

YOU KNOW that a great deal of fissionable material is missing and unaccounted for. We possess some of it. Enough of it to have created several small devices.

One of our devices has been constructed and is hidden in an abandoned uranium mine near Grants, New Mexico.

We are giving you forty eight hours to evacuate the human population within a hundred mile radius. At that point we will detonate this device in the mine unless all the nuclear powers have agreed to sit down and plan a complete world disarmament.

WE ARE SERIOUS. The detonation of this device in the abandoned uranium mine will send a plume of radioactive ore fragments thousands of feet in the air and may trigger earthquakes or even an eruption of Mt. Taylor.

STOP THE MADNESS OR WE WILL SHOW YOU THE DEPTHS OF YOUR EVIL!

THE TRINITY AVENGERS

Jed felt certain it would do the trick and the LANL letterhead was the icing on the cake. He mailed the letter from a box in the K-Mart parking lot, about as invisable a location as any in town.

Jed also started his fast that day, and in the evening Pajarito appeared at Jed's gate and announced, "The time has come. We leave for the sacred mountain tonight."

Jed and Lucy silently complied and in only a few minutes the necessary gear was stowed in the truck. They rolled out under a clear, starry canopy with an almost full moon rising over the dark contours of the Sangre de Cristo Mountains. Off on the dark opposite horizon the rising moon cast its light on another smaller massif. The gentle form of Mt. Taylor, Tzoodsix, sacred mountain of the south to the wandering people we call Navajo. One hundred miles west as an eagle flies, but already deep in the heart and mind of a young warrior.

Jed wanted to ask hundreds of questions as they rolled down the Interstate but the words would not come. The lights and traffic of Albuquerque brought Jed a little closer to present reality but that quickly faded as they climbed Nine Mile Hill and left the lights of the little city behind.

Somewhere around Canoncito, Jed finally spoke. "What if they don't believe the ransom letter? . . . Will I still dance? . . . I mean I couldn't . . . people could get hurt . . . I . . . "

Pajarito looked at Jed and raised his eyebrows.

"If they don't buy the warning then you didn't do a very important part of the dance correctly. And if any part of the harmony is off key then nothing will work. If they don't move the people all bets are off. We go home."

Jed decided that any more questions should be simple.

"Where are we going, Pajarito?"

"Get off at Laguna," he answered scratching his chin. "Then take old 66 through Cubero and San Fidel and almost to McCartys. Turn on to the old Rinconada Canyon Road. We'll hide your truck in the big trees by the river where Guadalupe Canyon comes into Rinconada."

Jed followed the instructions to the letter. A few miles up Rinconada Canyon the main Forest Service road crosses the stream and climbs out of the canyon and onto the ridge above San Fidel.

Just before the stream crossing Pajarito pointed straight upstream and said, "Go through that gate and stay on this side of the canyon."

Jed drove onto the two rut road and stopped at the wire ranch gate. "Its locked, Pajarito. There's a big heavy Master Lock on a log chain. We can't go in this way."

Pajarito looked thoughtfully through the windshield at the locked gate. "Well," he said slowly. "Let me have a look at it. I have a way with puzzles and locks."

The ancient old cacique shuffled through the head lights beam and over to the lock. He bent over and seemed to be speaking to it. As Lucy and Jed watched intently the old man stood up with the loose chain in his hand and smiled. He drug open the wire gate and pointed the way through for Jed.

Jed drove on past the gate and in his side mirror he watched Pajarito wrap the chain and hang the lock on the last link. They drove upstream on a rough track for about another mile to the confluence of Guadalupe and Rinconada Canyons. Jed squeezed his truck between tightly packed boxelders growing above the little streams.

As they stood in the splintered moonlight of the boxelder grove Pajarito seemed to be enjoying the sound of the flowing water. Finally he looked back down the road and put his hands on his hips.

"We better go wipe out our tracks to here before we go on up the mountain."

Jed nodded agreement with the suggestion and he headed out at a brisk rate for the gate. He was back inside of an hour sweeping the tire tracks and his own away with a juniper branch.

Lucy had all the gear packed and ready to go when Jed returned. He and Lucy shouldered their loads and began to follow Pajarito up the Rinconada Trail. They pushed on without rest for over five miles before Pajarito finally stopped and looked around at a sandy flat beside the stream under a complete canopy of riparian growth.

"This is where we will make a base camp."

There was no dissent among the sweaty hikers regarding the chosen location and a reasonably comfortable camp was soon established. The entire party laid on top of bedrolls and silently watched the dawn sky brighten through a leafy ceiling.

Before the new day was half over there were some definite signs of unusual activity in the skys above Mt. Taylor. A variety of aircraft were making systematic low level flights over the country around the mountain. It was obvious they were conducting a search and probably radiation surveys, looking for increased levels that might indicate the presence of a thermonuclear device. Occasionally the sound of sirens would waft up from the Interstate below. Jed smiled confidently. He was certain that the evacuation had begun.

As the soft light of twilight approached Lucy and Jed and Pajarito began a slow and cautious climb toward the peaks of the sacred mountain. Just below the summit a few lava columns rise from the slopes several hundred feet to form isolated pinnacles. Pajarito located and followed to the summit of one of pinnacles an ancient stairway carved in the basalt. At the top he showed Jed and Lucy a tiny rock shelter large enough for one or two people to sit in.

"This is a safe place for you to stay," he told Lucy. "The shelter is open to the sacred mountain so you will see all that occurs, but you will be protected if anything goes wrong."

From the summit of the pinacle the country to the south and east was visable for a hundred miles. Stretching along the ribbon of Interstate 40 like a ruby studded snake was a continuous line of traffic. There were no headlights pointing west, only the steady stream of evacuees heading east toward Albuquerque and away from the sacred mountain. It had worked. The ransom letter had worked and the people were leaving. This part of the dance was a success.

As the stars occupied the sky and the first glow of a full moon appeared behind the distant Manzanos, Pajarito spoke to Jed of the final preparations they needed to make. "It is time to prepare your body and mind young warrior. Come let's put on your paint."

Jed removed his clothes without question and tied his own breechcloth. Pajarito painted Jed's body with the white paint from the Rio Salado cave and with a black pigment. The colors were used about equally to cover his entire body, white on the left half and black on the right. Through the middle of his body, front and back, top to bottom Pajarito painted a bright yellow zig zag stripe.

"Now," The old man said as he finished the body paint. "We must prepare your mind a little better than at Sierra Ladrone. Lie down here on this flat stone." "Lucy," he said pointing to the rock shelter, "I will ask you now to enter this safe space and stay there until this thing is over."

Lucy hesitated a moment, looked at Jed, then slowly followed Pajarito's instructions.

Jed felt a little light headed from his fast as he lay on the flat stone near the center of the pinnacle. Pajarito walked up to him and placed the palm of his right hand over Jed's heart. Jed felt a sudden sense of warmth move through the trunk of his body and into his legs. Pajarito moved to Jed's head and held it between his hands. He turned Jed's head slowly and gently first to one side then the other. Then he suddenly snapped Jed's face back skyward.

Jed felt a jolt of what seemed like electricity run down his spine. He felt that his senses had been turned up to full capacity. His vision became crystal clear and his ears were picking up even the sound of the line of traffic far out on the distant Interstate. He also heard the distant rumble of thunder from the first line of storms of this year's monsoon.

Pajarito offered Jed a hand and helped him to his feet. As soon as they both were standing Pajarito seized Jed by the shoulder and looked directly into his eyes. Jed felt a crackling sensation on his skin and was amazed to see a bright yellow aura form around both he and Pajarito.

Pajarito pointed a glowing arm toward the summit of Tzoodsix and Jed knew it was time to begin the final climb.

Flashes of lightning and great rolls of thunder became more frequent as Jed and Pajarito began the climb from the base of the pinnacle to the summit of Tzoodsix. There was an end to the line of car tail lights out on the Interstate and the flashing lights of the police rear guard were slowly moving toward Albuquerque.

Jed felt absolutely clear and strong as he reached the highest point along the broad ridge that forms the summit of the sacred mountain. The brilliant full moon was almost directly overhead, but thin clouds moving in front of the approaching thunderheads were beginning to obscure the light. In the unreal light of the frequent lightning strikes Jed could see the pinnacle where Lucy waited. He did not allow his mind to be diverted to that place or that person.

Pajarito stood in front of Jed and looked sternly into his eyes. In a sudden movement Pajarito thrust both arms straight out from his shoulders, one palm down and one up. In an almost involuntary action Jed copied the stance except that his palms were reversed from Pajarito's. Immediately a bright band of electric color formed completely around the circle of the horizon.

Numerous multicolored strands of shimmering energy flowed from the circle of the horizon to Jed and Pajarito. These strands connected and merged with the brilliant yellow aura and formed an oblong envelope of dazzling color surrounding the two men. From under their feet more lines of crackling power diverged and ran across the mountain contours.

The canopy of raging thunderstorms crept closer to the mountain top and the frequent brilliant flashes added to the surreal quality of the scene. With the connection of all the lines of power rapid changes began to occur on the high ridge. The pulsating envelope of light surrounding Jed and Pajarito began to rotate, slowly at first but gradually increasing in speed until there was no visable distinction between the two men in the light enclosure.

From her position about a quarter mile separate from the summit ridge Lucy watched with amazement. The rotating and pulsating light envelope seemed to be making a deep roaring sound audible somehow even through the violent crashes of thunder. Lucy found herself beginning to fear for Jed's well being as the storms bore down on the mountaintop.

All of the lines of power and the light sphere containing Jed and Pajarito had been steadily increasing in size in direct proportion, it seemed, to the growing intensity of the storm. A thin platform of clear white light formed outward from the center of the shining envelope.

Suddenly, standing at points corresponding with the cardinal directions on the light platform, four kachinas appeared. Their masks and their body paint matched the color of the undulating rattlesnakes they each held.

The kachinas released their serpents, then followed them as they began to crawl toward the spinning central light. As the kachinas and the rattlesnakes were absorbed into the bright light it grew enormously in volumn and intensity. Simultaniously the storm hit in full force with frequent and violent lightning strikes all over the summit.

Lucy watched in fear and wonder from her tiny rock shelter on the lava pinnacle. The intensity of her experience bordered on sensory overload. Her love and fear for Jed were her thin line of physical reality that held her in present time and space.

As she watched and listened to the growing crescendo of natural and super natural phenomena she became gripped with fear and concern for Jed. In a wild moment of panic Lucy stood up in front of her safe shelter and vainly screamed Jed's name.

In the same moment a massive bolt of blue lightning crashed into the sacred mountain. A wave of sulferous gas and a deafening roll of thunder knocked Lucy from her feet. She landed back first against the overhanging rock of the shelter she had abandoned. Her head snapped backward and hit the rock hard. She slumped in a heap under the driving rain in a muddy spot in front of the rock shelter. All the world then wore the black and infinite cloak of nothingness. All of the struggle, and the pain, and the suffering and death, . . . all of the dramas and the love were overshadowed by the unconscious, empty shroud of nothing. For just a little while, maybe only a few seconds it seemed that the whole of earth existence was suspended in the great enveloping sea of the infinite. In those few crystaline moments of oneness, everything really was all right. It was for just that fleeting moment better than just affecting earth systems. It was beyond earth and everything else too for that matter. Everything, absolutely everything was for just an instant completely rendered neutral by the infinite nature of nothing. NO THING AT ALL.

When Lucy regained consciousness she was shivering under a fading night sky. The storms were gone and a clear morning sky was reddening to the east. She pushed herself up on one arm and wiped the mud from her face. Suddenly she remembered what had happened.

Lucy pulled herself to her feet and looked toward the summit of Tzoodsix. To be sure there were some morning mists shrouding the mountain, but clearly it had not erupted. The top of the mountain appeared scorched and there was no sign of Jed or any other life.

Lucy scrambled down the ancient stone stairway and started for the summit. She pawed her way up the muddy slope without regard for her own safety. Lucy could think of nothing but Jed and what may have happened. She slipped as she tried to run up the high ridge and slid about fifty feet down a muddy grade into a small ravine. Lucy was covered with cold mud and thoroughly exhausted but she began to claw her way back up.

When Lucy tossed her mud caked hair she noticed something move in the bottom of the ravine. As she looked closely at what appeared to be a muddy log she saw that it was in fact Jed. He was moving and moaning and alive.

Lucy ran to Jed and carefully moved her hands along his naked muddy limbs checking for breaks. He had no obvious serious injuries. Lucy lifted him up from the waist and held his head against her chest and began to cry. Jed opened first one muddy eyelid then another and looked at Lucy.

"Did it work?" he asked, then began to cough. "Did the mountain heal the land?" He asked again in a moment.

Lucy sighed and brushed Jed's mud caked hair with her fingers.

"No hostene . . . it didn't happen. Something went wrong and you're lucky to be alive."

"But how . . . ?" Jed started to ask before Lucy held her fingers to his lips.

"Hush now. There will be time for talking. Now we've got to get off this mountain and to a safe place."

Lucy helped Jed back to the base camp, pausing long enough to retrieve his clothes from the pinnacle. It was a slow and silent trip from the base camp back to the truck hidden in the boxelders.

Lucy drove cautiously over dirt reservation tracks from Rinconada Canyon to the Laguna settlement of Mogote and on even more obscure trails from there to Cabezon. She turned on the old radio but could find nothing but news of the nuclear terrorists and the evacuation of Grants and the odd series of earth tremors detected under Mt. Taylor the previous night. Jed was staring listlessly out of the truck window and did not speak the entire trip.

At her grandparents hogan Lucy carefully cleaned Jed then rubbed his head until he went to sleep in the bed of his truck. She spent the bulk of that day washing and cleaning her own wounds. In the late afternoon when Jed began to stir she brought him a steaming cup of Navajo coffee and a bowl of beans.

Jed took the nourishment slowly and without words. Lucy watched him with pity for a while then broke the silence.

"Jed . . . let's go for a little ride over to Cabezon and watch the sunset."

He did not respond immediately, but in a few moments he managed a tiny hint of a smile and nodded gently.

Lucy quickly caught two horses and saddled them while Jed stared at the distant massif of Mt. Taylor.

The two riders moved across snakeweed flats and through deeply incised arroyos to the base of the huge black volcanic neck called Cabezon. They tied their horses and climbed a timeworn trail to the top of this slain giants head.

The sun was touching the back of the sacred mountain as Jed and Lucy reached the summit of Cabezon. Bands of brilliant sunset color covered the sky from Mt. Taylor back to the Nacimientos.

Lucy watched Jed watching the sunset quietly and thought he seemed unable to look at her.

Finally, as the sun disappeared behind Mt. Taylor, Jed turned to his lover and his reason for life.

"Lucy," he began to speak slowly. "I made a terrible mistake. I tried to do something that was beyond my ability. I thought I could find a piece of the old magic . . . I thought I could be a cacique . . . I'm just a stupid white boy. I'm really sorry I got you involved in this craziness. I just wanted to stop the poison that killed your sister and her family. I wanted to believe it could happen. I'm sorry."

Lucy said nothing for a long while and Jed looked away again to the deepening sunset colors. As the deep pastels of the dying day crept across the landscape Lucy turned toward Jed and smiled.

"Hostene... my love... this was not a waste. Your quest was productive and powerful. You proved there is still enough of the old magic around to make life forever interesting. And in the course of that we found each other completely... our love became real."

Lucy folded her arms and shook back her hair. "But you know hostene," she continued, "you proved something else that's even more important. You proved that not even the residual power of a lost culture can reverse the destructive impact of the dominant culture. This is heavy shit for a profit driven culture to release the power of creation. They weren't ready to practice this kind of black magic and we're stuck with the legacy. The real lesson here is that no magic is gonna restore what we have poisoned with our greed. What we have to do now that we've learned the lesson is to do everything we can to stop the senseless madness... before this happens again... ever."

Jed raised his head and looked at Lucy. He smiled and held her close under the gathering twilight.

Lucy and Jed embraced on that black island in the sky and in their warmth and feeling for each other lay the seed of the one true and timeless magic. Life should be love and love should be abundant.

Where there is love, there is hope.

As night's sky deepened, out in the Puerco Valley, walking happily along, singing a little pueblo song, an old man smiled at the splender of this realm. Off in the arroyos coyotes yipped, and in a mud walled house beneath the sacred mountain a newborn baby found its mother's breast.

Life, splendid life, will continue.

THE END

CHAMISA DREAMS GLOSSARY

Anasazi. The Diñe (Navajo) term for the ancient ones, applied to pueblo Indians that left ruins at Chaco Canyon and smaller towns throughout the four corners area of the southwest United States.

Barrio. A spanish term for neighborhood, ward, or subdivision of a city.

Belagana. One of various spellings used in an attempt to anglicize the Diñe (Navajo) term for a white man.

Cabezon. A spanish term for a register of taxes paid to the government, colloquial in northern New Mexico, referring to a big head, or the giant head of Diñe (Navajo) mythology.

Cabezon, as referred to in *Chamisa Dreams*, is a volcanic plug or core which forms a prominent black butte in the valley of the Puerco River in north central New Mexico.

Cabrona. A spanish term for female goat. Cabrona is used colloquially in northern New Mexico, to refer to a very unpleasant and domineering woman, i.e. a bitch.

Cacique. A holy man or sorcerer among the Pueblo Indians of the American southwest.

Carne seca. A spanish term for dried meat or jerky.

Chaco Canyon. Location of the largest complex of Anasazi cultural remains known. Chaco Canyon is found in the central San Juan Basin of northwest New Mexico.

Chaco Mesa. The rough flat topped highland area east of Chaco Canyon and north of Mount Taylor in northwest New Mexico.

Chamisa. A common shrub component of plant communities in eroded stream bottoms in the U.S. southwest. A member of the composite family with thick feathery blue green foliage and clusters of yellow flowers in the fall.

Checkerboard lands. A pattern of land ownership and agency jurisdiction common in many parts of the United States southwest, wherein a section (640 acres or 1 square mile) of Navajo allotment land might adjoin a section of U.S. Bureau of Land Management land on one side, a section of New Mexico state land on another, an adjacent Navajo allotment at one corner and so on, giving a land ownership status map the look of a checkerboard.

Chindi. Diñe (Navajo) term for a malevolent spirit or ghost. Also spelled Chiindii.

Chuska Mountains. The largest mountain range on the Diñe (Navajo) Reservation stretching from north of Gallup, New Mexico to just south of the San Juan River near the Arizona-Utah border.

Commanche. A once powerful, southern plains buffalo culture tribe of Native Americans. Commanche culture is now almost completely absorbed into the dominant Anglo culture and other tribes.

Continental Divide. The topographic high point through a continent that separates drainage systems flowing to the opposite shores of the landmass. In the United States, the Continental Divide is the crest of the Rocky Mountains running generally north and south through the states of New Mexico, Colorado, Wyoming and Montana. In the United States, eastern slope drainages empty into the greater Atlantic Ocean via, for the most part, the Gulf of Mexico. Western slope drainages discharge into the Pacific Ocean, and in the U.S. Southwest via the Sea of Cortez, also known as the Gulf of California.

Diñe. An attempt to convert to English the term which the Native Americans we know best as Navajo (a spanish term) refer to themselves as. Roughly translated to English, it would mean The People.

Dos Equis. Mexican beer. Once confined in its United States distribution to the southwestern states, now widely available across the country.

El Malpais. Spanish, meaning the badlands. El Malpais, as it is referred to in *Chamisa Dreams*, is a large lava flow south of Mount Taylor that issued from a subsidiary vent called the Bandera Volcano. El Malpais is now the centerpiece of a National Recreation Area and federally designated wilderness in northwest New Mexico.

FAA. Federal Aviation Administration.

Fry bread. A deep fried batter bread perfected by the Diñe (Navajo).

Hogan. A traditional Diñe (Navajo) house. These structures are still widely used by the Diñe, though often in close conjunction with a house trailer or other modern dwelling that receives primary use. The exact construction materials and style vary considerably, but all hogans are essentially circular with a single east facing entry.

Hostene. Navajo term for a man. Various spellings may be found as with most attempts to render Diñe (Navajo) into English.

Huevos Rancheros. A spanish way of preparing eggs, where the eggs are covered with refried beans, cheese, chili and other spices in a sauce, all of which is usually smothering a corn tortilla.

Kachina. In the Hopi culture, Kachinas are messengers of the creator that dwell on the San Francisco Peaks and other mountains.

Kokopelli. A humpback flute playing figure often depicted in petroglyph panels throughout the four corners area. A popular character in Pueblo Indian mythology, often related to fertility.

Llano. A spanish term for the word plain.

Mesa Chivato. The flat topped highlands at the north end of the Mount Taylor highlands. The term chivato is a spanish term meaning a kid goat between 6 and 12 months of age.

Mesa Montanosa. An area of hilly, mountainous upland on Navajo checkerboard lands west of Mount Taylor in northwest New Mexico.

NAC. Native American Church, the peyote church. A Christian based religion practiced mainly by Native Americans that employs the hallucinogenic cactus, peyote, as a sacrament.

Nacimiento (as in Sierra Nacimiento or Nacimiento Mountains). Nativity, the beginning, the head of a river.

Norteno. A spanish term for a northern New Mexican native person of spanish ancestry.

Pajarito. A spanish term meaning a little bird.

Panniers. Packs, usually of canvas, that are suspended from a horse or mule pack saddle frame.

Paseo. A spanish term meaning the walk or the promenade. Colloquial in Santa Fe and other New Mexican towns, referring to a broad avenue that often encircles the town.

Patrona. A Spanish term, meaning the female boss.

Peyote. A small spineless cactus native to the lower Rio Grande drainage and various mountain ranges of Mexico. This cactus produces psychotropic alkaloids affecting the perception of humans who ingest it. This perception altering affect plays a key role in much Native American religious practice.

Puta. A spanish term for whore, prostitute, harlot.

Rito. A Spanish term meaning a little river or creek.

Roadman. The leader of a Native American Church ceremony.

San Mateo Mountains. The name given by the Spanish to two New Mexico mountain ranges. The relevant range to Chamisa Dreams being the highlands north of Mount Taylor in northwest New Mexico, the other being within the Greater Gila Ecosystem in southwest New Mexico.

Sand painting. A traditional Diñe (Navajo) depiction of deities and other power sources using different pigments of sand. The paintings are often created on the ground or floor of a hogan to promote healing or improve fortune.

Sangre de Cristo Mountains. Literally, the term Sangre de Cristo means the blood of Christ in the Spanish language. The Sangre de Cristo mountain range forms the southernmost part of the Rocky Mountains, and stretches from Santa Fe, New Mexico to Salida, Colorado.

Sierra Ladrone. A volcanic mountain range west of the Rio Grande in central New Mexico.

Tecate. Mexican beer. Once confined in its US distribution to the southwestern states, now widely available.

Tsoodzix. A European attempt to translate the Diñe (Navajo) term for the sacred mountain of the south, Mount Taylor. Also found with the spelling, Tsoodzill, and other various arrangements.

USGS. United States Geological Survey.

Yah ta hey. Diñe (Navajo) term for howdy!

CPSIA information can be obtained
at www.ICGtesting.com
Printed in the USA
LVOW07s0101020717
540103LV00001B/21/P